After the cold had seeped into our bones beyond the help of the blankets and heaters, we made our way back down to his room. It had been a night unrivaled by any I could remember. "Galaxies" had brought Beau and I together in the first place, so it only made sense that looking at the stars was the backdrop for the moment when I fell in love with him.

DREAMSPUN DESIRES

Dear Reader,

Love is the dream. It dazzles us, makes us stronger, and brings us to our knees. Dreamspun Desires tell stories of love featuring your favorite heartwarming heroes, captivating plots, and exotic locations. Stories that make your breath catch and your imagination soar.

In the pages of these wonderful love stories, readers can escape to a world where love conquers all, the tenderness of a first kiss sweeps you away, and your heart pounds at the sight of the one you love.

When you put it all together, you find romance in its truest form.

Love always finds a way.

Elizabeth North

Executive Director
Dreamspinner Press

Veronica Cochrane

Dance with Me

Published by
Dreamspinner Press

Published by
DREAMSPINNER PRESS

5032 Capital Circle SW, Suite 2, PMB# 279,
Tallahassee, FL 32305-7886 USA
www.dreamspinnerpress.com

This is a work of fiction. Names, characters, places, and incidents either
are the product of author imagination or are used fictitiously, and any
resemblance to actual persons, living or dead, business establishments,
events, or locales is entirely coincidental.

Dance with Me
© 2021 Veronica Cochrane

Cover Art
© 2021 L.C. Chase
http://www.lcchase.com
Cover content is for illustrative purposes only and any person depicted
on the cover is a model.

Paperback ISBN: 978-1-64108-293-8
Digital ISBN: 978-1-64108-292-1
Paperback published December 2021
v. 1.0

Printed in the United States of America
∞
This paper meets the requirements of
ANSI/NISO Z39.48-1992 (Permanence of Paper).

VERONICA COCHRANE is a contemporary m/m romance author. She penned her first story at age five, about her childhood best friend and a neighborhood cat. Many years later, she rediscovered her love of writing but is unfortunately no longer a feline enthusiast. Please don't hold that against her.

Veronica is an avid reader and a lifelong romantic. She loves seeing characters fall in love, overcome realistic obstacles, and find their happily ever after. When she's not writing, Veronica enjoys traveling to places with beautiful scenery, and seeing concerts and other live events. Veronica lives in Toronto, Ontario, with her husband.

Website: veronicacochrane.com
Twitter: @veronicacwrites
Email: veronicacochrane@outlook.com

By Veronica Cochrane

DREAMSPUN DESIRES
INEVITABLE DUETS
Next to Me
Dance with Me

Published by **DREAMSPINNER PRESS**
www.dreamspinnerpress.com

Acknowledgments

I AM so grateful for all the support I've received in this second visit into the world of the Inevitable Thorns. First, thank you to my husband for being incredibly supportive in this and every venture I pursue. Thanks to my friends and family for your encouragement and kind words. A huge thank you to the entire team at Dreamspinner Press for your dedication and help making this story become so much stronger than my original draft. Finally thank you to the reader for choosing to spend your time with characters I love so much.

(And no thanks to attention-hog Dean for commandeering a greater spotlight in this story than I had intended.)

Author's Note

I'VE always loved the concept of art bringing people together. Breathing new life into something classical or combining mediums that wouldn't normally blend together creates some wonderful surprises.

On paper, ballet and rock music are opposites, but the people behind them are often remarkably similar. Jamie and Beau are both passionate, dedicated, and creative individuals. The genres that define them are less important than the art that connects them. It was a pleasure writing their love story.

I hope you enjoy the journey.

With love,

Veronica

Beau

"**YOU** play keyboard most of the time, even when there's a full grand piano on the stage. Why?" Some preppy, glasses-and-button-down-wearing student in the middle asked me with his eyes full of condescension.

I thought about the question for a second, wanting to be honest about my answer but not blatantly insulting to all of the classically trained musicians in the lecture hall. I had agreed to talk to some freshmen as a favor to Chase, a good friend of mine who was an upperclassman in music composition at the Juilliard School. I never liked interviews much to begin with, and I had known going into this thing that my style of playing would be vastly different from what these kids were used to. The students at these types of private conservatories always seemed to have their noses in the air; however, Chase was adamant that the professor wanted to showcase the variety of career paths one could take in the music industry. I respected that, and seeing how Chase was basically the reason I wasn't a washed-up has-been before my twenty-fifth birthday, I was more than amenable to helping out when he approached me. That and I didn't have anything better to do today.

"Um, I guess it just suits me better? I'm not a classical pianist by any stretch of the imagination, and sitting behind a grand doesn't feel right to me most of the time," I answered. "There are a couple songs either Carter or I will play on the piano, but normally the keyboard is a better fit for me and also for our sound."

I was introduced to Chase through his boyfriend, my bandmate Carter West, earlier in the year. When our band, Inevitable Thorns, got back from our first national tour last spring, we struggled to write new music for our sophomore record. The four members of our group shared the songwriting responsibility, but we were all exhausted and were feeling the pressure to create music that lived up to the first release. We were ridiculously lucky that Chase came into our lives and stepped up, cowriting most of the songs that made the final cut. The album was absurdly well received, and our label immediately arranged for us to embark on an eight-month European circuit. A little over two months into the tour, it was going incredibly well, and we were having the time of our lives. However, we still faced some challenges.

Which is why we were here in New York now. Three days between gigs and Carter insisted upon hiring a private plane to fly us all across the Atlantic so he could see his guy. Carter was noticeably smitten with Chase, and fortunately it seemed like Chase was equally infatuated with Carter. It was sweet, really. They were perfect together, and I was exceedingly happy for them, yet seeing them so googly-eyed about each other made me wonder if I was missing out on something.

A couple more hands shot up, but the professor thankfully cut them off before I was forced to answer any more questions.

"I think that's all we have time for today. Thanks so much to Beau Davis for finding an hour in his busy schedule to join us. Class, remember your midterm paper is due in two weeks. Do *not* leave this one to the last minute."

The students shuffled—putting away notebooks and laptops, chatting with their neighbors as they left. I stuck around, and the professor and I made small talk for a minute or two. He began to pack up his things, so I thanked him again and headed for the exit. As I entered the adjoining hallway, I looked out the windows to see that it was absolutely pissing down rain outside. When Chase had walked me in, we'd entered through a hidden door in the courtyard that was right next to the classroom. Chase had already finished his classes and left, taking advantage of the few hours he had remaining with Carter.

I decided to cut through a hallway that looked like it led in the opposite direction, attempting to exit the building closer to the street, where I could hopefully catch a cab. The corridors had emptied quickly; it was getting late, and I figured most of the students were probably done for the day.

I made my way through the empty corridor for a while before realizing it curved around on itself and didn't appear to have an external door. Hearing music from the end of the hall, I decided to keep going in the hopes that someone could point me in the right direction. As I grew closer, I realized that it wasn't just any song that was playing, but one of Thorns's songs—the only one that I had written for our new album.

Before Chase had become involved, we only had a couple of usable tunes, one of which I had penned. The song was titled "Galaxies," and though it wasn't the most recognizable track on the sophomore record, it was meaningful to me, and our hard-core fans still knew the words by heart. When we played it in large theaters and stadiums, we encouraged the audience to shine the flashlights on their phones up at the stage. The vast auditoriums looked like they were filled with stars, and it was always a beautiful moment in the show.

I poked my nose into the room where the music was coming from, and my breath caught in my throat. A lone dancer flew through the air, graceful and perfectly in sync with the lyrics Carter sang. Reacting physically, I leaned in closer, completely in awe of the scene in front of me.

The dance studio itself was unassuming. A row of full-length mirrors covered one wall, with ballet barres lining the others, except for some space next to the door where there were shelves for students to store their things. A couple of posters above the shelves featured ballerinas in pointe shoes, with motivational sayings. The floor was black, and the ceiling was lofty, with speakers embedded high in the corners so you could hear the music from wherever you happened to be.

The dancer was breathtaking. He wore next to nothing—a simple pair of nude boy shorts that left very little to the imagination—but surprisingly his outfit wasn't what captured my attention. The lines of his body were so fluid as he progressed through the dance. His movements were impossibly complex. Yet he made them look effortless. He was wild but controlled. Purposeful though animalistic. Graceful and masculine. A jumble of contradictions that fought logic and gender norms in a beautiful display of dynamism. The power he radiated from every muscle and tendon was paralyzing.

The dancer's core was a perfect six-pack. His body was sculpted by practical use, not only for show, chiseled out of exercising for a living instead of hours spent ballooning at the gym. His legs extended each time he jumped; even his toes were stretching and pointing. His arms were long and elegant, holding tension and shifting around an invisible partner.

The piece was a duet. I could see that now from his movements. The passion he conveyed in every motion, every *breath*, was a fervent expression of desire. I had never been particularly enthusiastic about staged dance routines—they had always seemed dry and pompous to me, much like playing the piano instead of the keyboard—but the way this man showcased his body to a rock song shattered every preconception in my mind.

And it was *sexy*.

My God, the strength needed to lift and move himself so effortlessly captured my focus to the point that I didn't even notice when the music faded away and the song ended.

The dancer bent over and rested his hands on his knees. His chest rose and fell quickly as he fought to catch his breath from the vigorous feat. After a moment he stood and ran his fingers through his hair, drawing my attention to it. Despite his exertion the dancer's hair was still perfectly coiffed. It was the most beautiful color of mahogany red, longer on the top than the sides in a pompadour style. His locks were complemented by a well-maintained short beard that I had the immediate desire to feel scraping across my skin.

I shuddered involuntarily at the thought.

As he was already covered in a light sheen of sweat, it didn't take much to slot this man into the fantasy category. His intense blue eyes flickered up in the mirror, sensing my presence and, embarrassingly, noticing me drooling over him. Despite the feeling of being caught with my hand in the cookie jar, I couldn't force myself to look away. A crease furrowed his brow as he turned to face me, replaced a second later by a look of recognition.

"Holy shit, you're Beau Davis," he told me.

While I had grown somewhat accustomed to being recognized in public, it was never as frequent for me as it was for Carter, or when I was out with a second band member. It still threw me off a little when it happened. It was weird that people knew who I was. With overly enthusiastic fans, I had a hard time deciding exactly how I should react. In general, I mostly kept to myself, preferring to relax with a book or a movie after a concert instead of tracking down parties and groupies with my bandmate Dean.

"I am." I chuckled out loud at his assessment. "Sorry for barging in. I got lost and heard music down the hall. That was… wow… that was amazing," I said, struggling to adequately express how moved I was by what I had seen.

His blue eyes sparkled, and he grinned at me. He moved closer to the doorframe I had somehow become glued to.

"Thank you. It's still a work in progress. Obviously. But that's so cool you liked it. I'm Jamie, by the way." He extended his hand for a shake.

It was such a simple gesture—the smallest, most mundane amount of contact. Nonetheless, feeling his skin for the first time gave me butterflies. His hands were smooth and soft, unlike my own calloused musician's hands. I caught myself staring at our joined hands, feeling a little slow because of his touch.

"Oh, sorry," he said, looking down at the expanse of his bare chest, likely assuming that was what I was gaping at.

Now that he'd drawn my attention to it, I couldn't take my eyes off his torso. Jamie plucked a T-shirt off of the floor and pulled it over his head at leisure, seemingly unbothered by his own nakedness. I looked up to meet his gaze, pretending I hadn't been ogling him.

"So what are you doing here at Juilliard?" He asked.

I forced myself out of my stupor, trying to focus and be a coherent conversationalist.

"Oh, um, I was a guest at one of the first-year music classes. A favor to a friend of mine," I replied, still feeling sluggish and stupidly affected by this stranger in front of me.

"Cool. The students must have loved having you," he said, smile easy and warm.

"I dunno about that." I laughed. "I think I'm a little too rough around the edges for the Juilliard crowd."

"Some of us like it rough." He winked at me.

My face got hot from his blatant flirting; I had no idea how to respond. No way did he know how accurate that statement was. Right?

"But seriously," Jamie continued, smirking at my flustered reaction, "they need a shake-up when they first get here. They're always too classical. Too focused on the rules. Nothing great comes out of simply copying what someone else does."

The unexpected profoundness of Jamie's statement affected me. I had never been formally trained or had aspirations to be any type of prim and proper musician. Not that there was anything wrong with that; it just wasn't who I was or a part of the opportunities I had been given in life. Ever since I'd walked into the building earlier, I had felt *less than*. Less than trained. Less than classy. Less than part of the elite—which was ridiculous, because I made more money and had more fans than I knew what to do with. Yet I couldn't help but think back to a time when that hadn't been the case.

It had been a weird day all around.

"Hey, so I'm sure you've got stuff to do, and you probably get this all the time, but any chance I can buy you a drink and ask you a few questions about your music?" Jamie asked. "There's a couple bits of this piece I'm struggling with, and it would be amazing to get your opinion." He ran a towel over his face and began throwing his stuff into a bag.

Something about Jamie was calling out to me. Obviously he was gorgeous, but I was drawn to him for other reasons I couldn't fully describe. I had no idea why I was so fascinated by him. All I knew was there was no way I was going to pass up a chance to spend more time in the company of this captivating man.

"I'm not much of a dancer. Not sure I'd be any help." I smiled self-consciously. "But yeah, I've got some time."

Jamie

"YOU didn't!" Beau exclaimed, laughing uninhibitedly over the top of his second beer.

"Totally did. So after I came offstage, the costume designer and the director called me over and chewed my ass off about the changes I made to my outfit. They *did* stop short of firing me on the spot—probably because they didn't want to teach someone else the part overnight. But the review in the *Times* the next day specifically raved about how my outfit was the perfect dramatic paradox—that's what they said: "dramatic paradox"—for the piece. Long, *long* story short, that plus an injury made me decide that telling people what to do is way better than being told. Creating my own shit is more fun than dancing the stuffy old *Nutcracker* every year for eternity."

"So you became a choreographer," Beau concluded.

"So I became a choreographer." I nodded. "And now those pretentious pricks keep me employed because I do my job well and they're terrified of me leaving to go work for another company. Plus they take care of the boring admin crap like getting the licensing rights to use the music, so I can't complain too much."

I paused to take a sip of my drink. "Ballet isn't just classical pieces anymore. It can be modern. Lyrical. Emotional and exciting. Contemporary dance is every bit as important as the *Swan Lakes* of the world. It makes people feel and connect. Sometimes it's easier to express yourself and tell a story with movement instead of words."

Yes, I was aware I probably sounded cocky as fuck to the Grammy-winning, world-class musician sitting beside me on his bar stool, but I couldn't help it. Talking about dance—especially my type of dance—brought out the passion in me, and it was hard to remember to tone it down when I got on a roll.

"Wow, that's amazing. Now that you mention it, I vaguely remember going through the music rights for stuff like that with our agent. Guess I hadn't really thought about it. I had no idea people actually do, like, choreography to Thorns's songs. Dancing at a club or something, yeah. But what you did in there? That was something else." Beau's soulful brown eyes were wide.

Tonight was a trip. I had no idea how I'd ended the night in my local bar talking to this crazy-talented man. Inevitable Thorns was one of my all-time favorite bands. I had choreographed to a couple of their pieces over the years. Their music seemed to lend itself perfectly to the way I liked to create movement: fluid, with an intensity behind it. Melodic but filled with edge and angst. The Thorns songs were filled with stories of love and tragedy, more akin to opera than a lot of the crap on the radio today.

The piece I had been working on earlier was one of the lesser-known songs on their latest album. That was another thing I loved—not sticking to the single or the obvious choice for the music. It was like bringing new life to a piece that might be forgotten over time. "Galaxies" was just as deserving of accolades as any of Thorns's bigger hits, but there were simply too many good tracks in their catalog for all of them to become sensations.

"I'm really happy you liked it. Like I said, it's still a work in progress."

I raised my glass to my lips to take a gulp of the cool liquid.

"Can I ask you something?" I asked, not wanting to squander the opportunity to talk to Beau about his music. He nodded and gestured for me to go on. "So I guess I'm just trying to figure out how to play the ending. It's so ambiguous in the final verse. I know that he leaves his lover because of the hurt she's caused, but there's still hope there too. Does that mean she eventually gets better? Do they find their way back to each other?"

He smiled at me, seemingly enjoying listening to my interpretation of the lyrics his band had written.

"What?" I finally asked. I furrowed my brow, self-consciousness getting the best of me. "I'm not that far off, am I?"

"No, not far off." Beau stroked his chin before continuing slowly. "I guess I don't really know about the ending. I did need to leave to get out of a bad situation, but I'm always optimistic that the other person will eventually find their way. Not so we can be together. For themself. So it *is* kind of ambiguous, in my mind at least. The listener can interpret it as either cautiously hopeful for the future or the end of the relationship."

I thought for a moment about that unhelpful comment. Vagueness wasn't the worst thing in the world, but I wished Beau had a clearer answer. There was something about the piece that called out to me. I got the sense that I was circling the spark, the magic. It seemed to be just outside my grasp, but I couldn't put my finger on what exactly *it* was.

"But, um… it's not about a she," Beau added quietly. "At least it wasn't when I wrote it."

I paused for a second, genuinely caught off guard.

"Oh shit, seriously?" I asked. "You're gay?"

"Bi, actually. But this song was about a guy. I didn't, like, purposely leave out pronouns or anything, they just didn't work into the lyrics. I kinda liked how it turned out, not weighed down by answers or concrete details. Or gender. It's not a song that gets talked about much, so nobody's really asked us during interviews or anything."

Egoistically I was far more engrossed by the new ideas this admission generated for my choreography than about Beau's personal confession. Even before I consciously thought it through, I knew immediately that this was the flame I had been looking for. My head was spinning.

The piece I had been creating was a typical duet between a man and a woman. I had already mentally cast the male lead, but I was having a hard time deciding who the female should be. This revelation offered the opportunity to change things.

I suddenly felt alive with possibility. My blood pumped rapidly through my body, thumping loudly in my ears. The skin on my arms grew tight with goose bumps, and my whole body vibrated with the creative energy that was flowing. Now that the idea was embedded, I couldn't picture the number as a traditional male/female pas de deux anymore.

It needed to be danced by two men.

Fuck.

It *needed* to be danced by two men.

It would be a lot of work to change things, but I immediately knew the guy I wanted to cast in the second role. The jumps and partnering work came alive in my head. A homage to masculine strength and capacity, both in their dance and in their relationships. I was practically spilling over with ideas, each newly conceivable combination coming together rapidly in my mind.

Holy shit. This piece had instantly gone from fine to fucking fantastic.

Modern lyrical pieces between two men were still absurdly rare, mainly due to the overall emphasis on female ballerinas and conventional partnering in the dance world. Men were naturally heavier to lift and didn't usually receive the training to be lifted in the way that women did. The grace and emotionality were different between genders in dance. Not that men weren't graceful or emotional in their performances; it was just different. This was an opportunity to show that off.

I had wanted to create a work on two guys before, but this was the perfect piece of music for it. And the fact that the song left the gender of the lovers ambiguous made it even more interesting.

"Jamie? Are you okay?" Beau asked, peering at me intently. "You're kind of staring off into space. That's not a problem for you, is it? That I'm bi?"

"Hmm?" I tried to refocus my attention on Beau's confession of his own sexuality instead of on the miniature dancers running around in my head. "No, oh God, of course not. I'm gay. I was, like, thinking about what that meant for my piece. Super selfish, I know."

I laughed awkwardly, hoping he didn't think I was the most narcissistic person on the planet. My world was centered on dance. Most people outside of the industry didn't understand that, though I supposed a musician would get it better than most.

Even though I was an Inevitable Thorns fan, I'd had no idea Beau was bi. It didn't seem like he was out publicly, not that I had any right to judge him for that. I tended to run a little flirty with everyone, although now that I was thinking about it, I had definitely been getting a vibe from him since we started talking back in the studio.

Fortunately after a second, Beau laughed too.

"Not selfish at all. I was cocky to assume you were thinking about me," he said with a shy smile.

"Thinking about you is certainly no hardship." I tested the waters a little with a wink.

His eyes flared for a brief heartbeat. Oh yeah, he was definitely feeling the same electricity I was. I held his gaze but changed the subject, not wanting to push him too far too fast. Plus I was still curious to dive deeper into the meaning of the song.

"So tell me about the guy," I prompted. "You're not with him anymore, I take it, based on the ending?"

"Nah," he responded casually.

It helped me to relax a little knowing I wasn't stepping in the middle of some epic love story.

"I don't know if we were ever really together in the first place in his eyes. It was more the idea of him than anything. Tall, dark, mysterious, and handsome. Someone you want to try to save but who doesn't want to save himself. It gets old eventually."

"I'll drink to that." I raised my glass in a toast before taking a small sip of my drink, not wanting to get buzzed and embarrass myself. I don't usually drink much; the empty calories never felt worth it to me. As a result my tolerance for booze of any kind was pathetically low. My body had taken a hit since I stopped dancing professionally, and it took more effort to keep myself in shape when I wasn't working out constantly.

"It was a long time ago now. I tour too much for anything serious," Beau said.

"Not serious can be fun," I teased, putting more of my cards on the table.

Reaching out, I ran my finger lightly over his knee.

He closed his eyes. His lips parted a little, and he pulled his lower lip between his teeth, biting down ever so slightly. Beau was the dictionary definition of sensuous at that moment. He was so effortlessly sexy. It was like he was fighting his natural urges to give in to the pleasure I was offering, but then he wasn't quite strong enough to deny himself entirely. God, I wanted him.

My mind went into overdrive, picturing a scenario where we were back in the dance studio he'd found me in. Beau had that exact look on his face as he leaned against the barre while I sank to my knees. He held my head, running his fingers through my sweaty hair, watching our reflection in the various angles of the ballet mirrors while I went down on him.

"So, um," he started, voice gravelly before clearing his throat and bringing me out of my fantasy. My hand was still on his thigh, stroking up and down along the inseam of his jeans near his knee. Nothing too aggressive, just enough to let him know I was very, very interested and the proverbial ball was in his court.

"I fly out again in the morning, back to Europe for the tour. But my place isn't too far from here." His voice trailed off at the end in suggestion as he looked up at me expectantly.

Beau's adorable self-consciousness at the proposal gave me the impression he didn't do this nearly as much as he could, given his profile. Something about Beau's demeanor from the time we met—had it only been a few hours now?—called out to me. Shy was the wrong word to describe Beau Davis. Maybe a word more like… pensive? Introverted?

He played his cards close to his chest, observing instead of saying a lot. There was intelligence behind his eyes and a depth to him. Perhaps some self-preservation. I knew that if anything happened between us, it wouldn't be long-term. As much as I was all for casual sex, I tried to ignore the fact that something about this whole situation felt cheaper than either of us deserved. But given the circumstances, I couldn't deny that I was incredibly attracted to Beau, and I certainly was not going to be the one to say no to his offer.

A couple of bills from my wallet covered the tab and a tip for the bartender. I swallowed the last sip of my beer quickly and hid my internal doubt with a cocky grin.

"Give me two minutes and I'm yours, rock star," I said with a wink.

Beau

WHAT the fuck had gotten into me? I never hooked up with random strangers. I especially never invited them into my home for what would unmistakably be a one-night stand. Even before the success of the Thorns, bringing someone home with me was such a rare occurrence that I could probably count the number of times I had done it on a single hand. I liked my privacy, and the thought of inviting a person I barely knew into my apartment made me cringe. But with Jamie the words were practically out of my mouth before I realized what I was saying. To make matters worse, I don't think I would have taken them back if I could have. I wanted this. Wanted him. And that thought was the one that was freaking me out more than the others.

I had no uncertainty in my mind about what this was. Jamie was incredibly good-looking, and he had a body I would worship with my tongue if he would let me. Nonetheless it was only a hookup, and I understood that.

So I gave myself a mental pep talk. We would have one night together, and no matter what happened, I would not—*would not*—dwell on it after it was over. I had a bad habit of getting more attached than I should, a fact that embarrassed me to no end and was something that I worked to keep hidden from those around me. Hell, the song that brought Jamie and me together in the first place was proof positive that my inability to let people go was possibly my greatest character flaw. Even if those people hurt me.

Especially if they hurt me.

Dylan, the guy I had written "Galaxies" about, had been the center of my world for nearly two years. I had downplayed the whole thing to Jamie, as I did with almost everyone. Oblivious to the truth, I had crushed on Dylan and been on-and-off with him for far too long. It took me forever to realize that I was ultimately enabling him to continue descending down the spiral of drug and alcohol abuse he was poisoning himself with. I thought it was love—fate or destiny or whatever—but to him I was merely a convenience. Someone he could easily take advantage of emotionally and financially. My father had many of the same issues as Dylan, which is probably why Dylan's problems never seemed to stand out as red flags as much as they should have.

Carter was the only person I had ever been completely honest with about my plight with my ex. I started writing "Galaxies" when I was still caught up in the vortex—as a way to figure out my feelings—but the song was only finalized after Dylan and I were officially done. I hadn't been lying to Jamie about the ending to the song. While Carter had finally talked enough sense into me to enable me to break free of the murky cycle with Dylan, I had no idea what had happened to Dylan since. I wanted good things for him, but I needed to close that chapter. Letting Dylan go gave me a sense of power over my life, and as difficult as it was to walk away, it was still far easier than addressing the underlying, mirrored issues with my father. For some reason, hopeless entanglements were the relationships I naturally seemed to gravitate to. I tried to fix people, but it always seemed to be me that got hurt in the end.

As unhealthy as it may have been, casual sex seemed like a better alternative than allowing my brain to pull me into the dark tailspin of being alone tonight. Staying emotionally detached was my priority.

"Ready?" Jamie asked, appearing next to me after returning from the men's room.

The foggy memory in my mind was instantly gone, and my focus returned to the dazzling creature beside me. I nodded, gesturing for him to go in front of me so we could navigate through the narrow gap between the bar and some tables. It was too dark to get much of a view, but my gaze instinctively dropped downward to watch how his jeans gently hugged his drool-worthy ass. Jamie chose that instant to open the door and hold it for me, thereby noticing me blatantly checking him out. He smirked knowingly. I shrugged and grinned back at him, not feeling guilty in the least for being caught staring. He was hot, and we both knew exactly where this was going.

The rain had stopped, and it was dark outside now, indicating exactly how long we had spent shooting the shit inside the bar. Hooking up should be the last thing on my mind, considering how damn early my flight was the next morning, but I couldn't bring myself to care at this particular moment. That was tomorrow-Beau's problem.

As we exited, I meant to steer us left and walk the five or so blocks to my Hell's Kitchen condo. But before I could, Jamie sidetracked us, tugging at my arm and pulling us into a narrow redbrick alleyway between the bar and the next building over. His cobalt eyes darkened predatorily as his body backed mine against the cold, rough brick siding.

"God I've wanted to do this all night," he said softly, probably more to himself than to me.

His hands cupped my jaw. An electric pulse shot between us like nothing I had ever experienced before. We were pressed together so tightly in the small alcove I could feel every bump and ridge of his lithe frame. I was encompassed by the warmth he radiated, despite the October chill and lingering dampness. His well-groomed beard prickled against my cheeks as I had imagined it would. I swear to God I whimpered as he leaned in and ran his tongue slowly along my lower lip. Without a conscious thought, I immediately opened for him as he all but demanded entry into my mouth, taking the kiss from merely a possibility to an eleven in a single heartbeat. I tried desperately to hang on for the ride as he mercilessly sucked on my tongue, leaving me a moaning and quivering mess within seconds. It was without a doubt the single hottest kiss of my life. As somewhat of a public figure—even one that didn't get recognized on a daily basis—maintaining my privacy was important to me. But here I was, barely masked by the night and the shadows, getting kissed within an inch of my life by someone I had known for a few short hours.

My hands found Jamie's lower back, and I pulled him even closer to me. I felt the swell of his erection rubbing against the mirroring ridge in my own jeans, which had quickly become too tight. He slipped his leg between mine. I gasped into his mouth at the increase in the mind-blowing friction that created.

A door slammed somewhere down the alley, making us both jump.

I turned my head away from the sound, shielding my face from view. Sensing my reaction, Jamie pushed his body even more into mine, protecting my identity from anyone who happened to notice or care. That small gesture—however unnecessary—was not lost on me, and I relaxed against him.

"Sorry," Jamie said with a chuckle, his voice deep and husky. "Got a little carried away." He reached down slyly and adjusted his jeans.

I laughed, breaking some of the lingering tension of the moment. "Definitely have nothing to be sorry for there," I said, snapping up his lower lip between mine one more time. "If you can wait ten minutes till we get to my place, I'm sure we can find some other things not to be sorry about."

He rubbed his jaw thoughtfully, teasing me. "Ten minutes is an awfully long time."

We walked quickly and made it in nine.

Jamie

THE instant the lock on Beau's fourth-floor walk-up clicked, we were on each other again. I pinned his back against the door, as if to resume from where we'd left off outside the bar. We had each other spun up again in seconds. Grasping and tugging on fabric, clawing at each other to get as close as possible. The fire that had been simmering all night wasn't just smoldering anymore. It was an inferno, swirling and radiating around us in a cyclone of heat, threatening to engulf both of us in flames. I had initiated our first kiss in the alley, unable to keep my hands off the hot-as-sin musician for a moment longer. He was the instigator now, owning my mouth with his kiss. His hands skirted over my still-clothed body like they couldn't get enough. Like they wanted to possess me.

And *holy hell*, this man could kiss. It was sloppy and messy. Unrefined. Desperate. It was like any sort of practiced technique went out the window in favor of devouring me.

He suddenly dropped to his knees, reversing the fantasy I'd concocted of us in the dance studio. Fuck, we hadn't even made it out of the entryway yet, had we? My head fell backward in lust as my heart hammered in my chest. It felt like I had just completed a leading role in one of Neumeier's grueling marathon ballets. I couldn't seem to catch my breath. The throbbing heat between my legs bordered upon painful as Beau popped the button on my jeans. He looked up at me innocently through his long eyelashes, his brown eyes silently asking for permission to continue.

"Yeah, baby. You can suck it," I told him with a soothing tone, cupping his soft cheek.

He moaned loudly, unambiguously turned on by my words. His hands glided over my ass; he slipped my jeans over my hips and dragged them down my thighs. Then he hooked his thumbs into my nude shorts and dance belt and pulled both down in one motion, finally freeing my aching member.

"Oh fuck." He groaned, rubbing my cock over his smooth face. Worshipping it. Evidently Beau was a guy who loved sucking dick, and who the hell was I to deny him that? I bet you couldn't find a man alive who didn't feel like a king when his lover craved his manhood like that.

"That's it, baby. You can have it. It's all for you," I cooed.

I carded my fingers through Beau's dark blond locks before pulling him gently toward me, encouraging him to take me between his beautiful, candy-pink lips. I

kept my hands on either side of his head, holding him in
place. He could easily move if he wanted to, but I was
getting the sense that my little rock star liked things a
bit rough.

Beau swirled his tongue around the dripping wet
head while staring straight into my eyes. He sighed
deeply, like it was the sweetest treat he had ever tasted,
while I practically yelled out from gratitude. I watched
my cock be enveloped in the vacuum of Beau's mouth
as he sucked me down slowly, an inch at a time. Fuck.
His plump lips finally kissed my short, ruddy curls as
he swallowed the last of my length, drinking me all in.
I slipped into his throat for a split second, gasping at the
feeling of his muscles massaging me. While I wasn't
exactly a porn star, my cock had a challenging curve
and seeing him eat it so easily made my already-tight
balls lift a little higher. It had clearly been far too long
since I had gotten laid. I was already getting close and
we had barely even started yet.

Pulling back a little, Beau steadied himself by
holding the flesh of my ass. He tugged my hips toward
him, his lips strained around me, and… oh hell, he
wanted me to do the work, didn't he? Goddamn this
man was pressing every single one of my buttons.
Holding back a groan, I sank my teeth into my lower lip
instead. I took over the blow job, fucking myself in his
mouth. Keeping things gentle to begin with until I was
certain he could handle more, I held his head between
my hands and slowly pushed into the mind-blowing
suction he was giving me.

"God, that's right, Beau. You're doing so good."

He groaned and sucked me harder, doubling down
after the praise, eager for more. My thrusts picked up
speed, becoming deeper and more punishing. Beau's

eyes watered and saliva ran down his chin, but he clung to my hips, forcing me to keep using his throat like he never wanted me to stop. His moans created the most incredible vibrations.

I edged him backward so his head was completely trapped between the door and my hips. He had absolutely nowhere to go and could do nothing but take the hard cock I was giving him. I smacked my right hand against the unyielding oak to brace myself as my left continued to massage Beau's stretched jaw. Using him for my pleasure, I felt the familiar sparks at the base of my spine, growing and building in intensity.

"Fuck. I need to come, baby. Can I come in your mouth?" I panted frantically.

He groaned something that sounded positive around his mouthful, grappling at my ass to make sure I didn't pull out.

I snapped my hips faster and faster, losing the rhythm when all I could think about was burying myself into his throat. My eyes squeezed closed of their own accord as hot come erupted like lava through the length of my cock and poured into Beau's mouth. I stroked up and down his neck with my thumb, feeling the muscles work to swallow all my juice as I fed him shot after shot. My voice grew raw from screaming out my pleasure, and my spine went liquid from the intensity of the orgasm. I gasped for air, pulling breaths into my overworked lungs. When I hit the point of oversensitivity, I slipped my softening cock from Beau's swollen lips, staring intently into his eyes, which remained crazy with lust. I looked down and saw the last drops of my come dribbling out from the side of his mouth. His hair was all over the place from the assault of my fingers; his hardness still tented his pants.

He looked utterly debauched and yet frantic with need for his own release.

I sank down hurriedly, propping Beau up against the door and positioning myself between his kneeling legs. My hands flew to undo his belt buckle and pull his jeans over his hips. The front of his plain black boxer-briefs was soaked with precome, wet to the point I wasn't convinced he hadn't already lost his load. His head drooped over my shoulder, his wrecked voice howling with need. I didn't even have time to admire his long, elegant cock before swallowing it down. The angle was awkward but nonetheless I had barely gotten him into my mouth when his whole body started to shake. He cried out in anguish as I felt the first bursts of his release hit the back of my throat. Beau's hands forced my face into his crotch to take every last bit of pleasure he could get from my tongue.

Some people would be turned off by the fact that Beau had gone off so fast, but Christ, seeing him so worked up from blowing me got my pulse racing all over again. He finally slumped against me, and we both sat there for a second, utterly depleted from our orgasms. My head was still in his lap, his fingers spread in my hair.

"Fuck," he finally said. "I needed that."

He met my gaze, and the sides of his eyes crinkled with mirth. We both burst out in giggles simultaneously, catharsis from the intensity of the past half hour. I buried my face in his thigh in an attempt to control the laughter.

"You hungry?" Beau asked.

I nodded, smiling giddily up at him.

Beau

WHAT did one do after having the most intense orgasm of his life with a perfect stranger when he had to leave for the airport in approximately five hours? Offer to make midnight pancakes, of course.

By all accounts I should find an excuse to get Jamie to leave and then try to get a few hours of sleep before my flight to Berlin. Hell, a sane person probably wouldn't have invited a hookup over in the first place. But Lord help me if I could find an ounce of regret for what had transpired, or if I had any intention of seeing Jamie out a moment earlier than absolutely necessary.

I honestly wasn't sure what had gotten into me tonight. Maybe I had been possessed by some type of horny alien or something. While I certainly had indulged in fantasies of having aggressive sex, "vanilla" was probably the word that my past partners would have used to describe their encounters with me. But the mental loop of me dropping to my knees and all but begging Jamie to fuck my throat told another story.

Though I considered myself to be bisexual, it had been a while since I had hooked up with a guy. Actually, I knew exactly how long. Take the night I finally ended things with Dylan and add three days to it. That's how long. Consciously or subconsciously, I had been avoiding that part of myself for a while and the solid feel of a man's body tonight reminded me what I had been missing. And to have such an emphatically male experience only added to it. Tonight would be jerk-off material for the rest of the tour, easily.

I flipped the last pancake onto the plate.

"So, how did you and the guys from Thorns meet?" Jamie asked as we dove into our tasty snacks.

"We all went to high school together, actually," I said, trying to not use the exact same language as we used in a million interviews. "Both Carter and I come from military families. His dad got transferred right before our senior year. He wasn't used to being the new kid, but my family moved around all the fucking time. I wasn't exactly the most popular kid in school, so I helped show him around until he got his footing. We ended up bonding over music, realized we both played instruments and liked the same kinds of bands. Cart befriended Ash, who was also kind of an outsider, and Dean saw the three of us jamming one day in the cafeteria after school and fucking decided to invite himself to join in. Never played drums before in his life, but I guess he saw an opening and started hammering on some lunch tables with a couple of Sharpie markers." I chuckled at the memory.

"Eventually we realized we weren't gonna shake Dean, so we convinced Ash—who plays every instrument known to man—to switch from rhythm guitar to drums. We threw Dean the simplest instrument we could think of, the bass guitar, and he was a little less pathetic at that."

Jamie threw his head back in laughter. It was a glorious sound. I loved my band brothers, but Dean deserved every inch of teasing he got. He knew he wasn't the most gifted musician out there, but Thorns certainly wouldn't be the same without his constant hijinks.

"That's so great," Jamie said. "I can totally picture Dean with the Sharpies."

"Yeah, that story's become somewhat of an urban legend," I agreed, nodding. "When Dean's signing autographs with Sharpies, he'll normally get at least one fan that points it out. He loves it, though—plays it up, and sometimes he'll even sign a pen for the fan."

"Did you always wanna be a musician?"

"I hadn't really figured it out, to be honest. Maybe amateurly? My family wasn't exactly well-off, so I probably would have gone into something more secure. Most kids in bands dream about this, but I don't think I ever imagined making a living off of music. Cart was so damn excited when he started getting us shitty little gigs it was hard to say no. It kinda spiraled from there. None of us would have predicted playing at this level. Well, except Carter maybe." I shook my head at my crazy bandmates and the life we had somehow created for ourselves.

"That's really sweet. And you and Carter never… you know?" He raised his eyebrows in an unasked question.

When Inevitable Thorns first started, we played this depressing gig that had less than twenty people in this scuzzy little club. The club wasn't paying us, so they let us drink for free; they may or may not have known we were underage. All four of us got absolutely shitfaced as soon as we left the stage. Dean and Ash both fucked off, leaving Carter and me alone to commiserate at the bar. We were both barely coherent, and I got the genius idea to put my hand on his thigh. Carter's always been a good-looking guy. He never seemed to date or be interested in any of the girls who threw themselves at him. As we had gotten to know each other better, I began to wonder what his deal was and if I maybe had a shot. Intraband romances are never a smart idea, but I was young and horny and… not smart.

And drunk. Very, very drunk.

Anyway, the poor asshole had clearly been struggling because as soon as I started to move my fingers a little, his big, wide, Disney-princess eyes started leaking, and before I knew it, the sap was crying like a hunter shot his mother. I spent the next two hours holding him while he blubbered over the guy that got away. I didn't find out until we had sobered up the next day that Cart had literally never told anybody that he was gay before. Cut to almost five years later, he and Chase are about two gumballs short of Candy Land with the tooth-rotting sugary cloud that permeates the air between them.

"Hooked up?" I finally answered. "Nah. I might have thought about it once or twice when Cart and I first met, but he's only ever had eyes for Chase."

We ate through companionable, light chitchat, finishing our pancakes and going back and forth with surface questions. I found myself enjoying Jamie's company. It was easy with him, not at all awkward or like I was being taken advantage of for my fame. Jamie was definitely a fan, but not an obsessive, hide-in-your-dressing-room type fan.

As the conversation wound on, I became more aware of the hour, and as much as I had been avoiding it, my mind started to shift back to the flight that was growing closer and closer. Eventually our yawns grew wider, our words slower, and Jamie decided to call it a night. I walked him to the door. Long before the first rays of the sun began flirting with the horizon, after a parting kiss and a wink, he left.

Jamie

"**FIVE,** six, seven, eight. And one, two, and three, four, five, six, seven, and eight. Good! Now, Reece, you're going to stay in the center and extend from there into a second arabesque. Reach for him like you're desperate. You'll die if he doesn't come back to you. Good, watch the line of your back leg. It's emotional, but don't lose the technique. Yes, yes, perfect! And Hayd, you're going to make a full circle around him with a series of grand jetés and barrel-roll turns. It's like you're losing control and he can't keep up with you. Watch what I do here, and then you can try it."

I demonstrated what I meant a few times slowly before trading places with my dancer. It was always an electric moment: watching the piece I'd been sculpting in my mind begin to come together before my eyes.

We had about another month to get it perfect for the first-term showcase, which led the students into their Christmas break. It was becoming an extraordinary number, unquestionably the best of my career to date. It was also the kind of work that might even make my pretentious-as-fuck colleagues see the value in keeping modern choreographers like me on staff. And it was all thanks to a random encounter with the single hottest man I'd ever met.

It was impossible not to think about Beau Davis when I was working on this piece. He was laced into every line of the song, every heartbeat. Not only his beautiful words but all of his being. Beau was the character Reece was playing. Urgently begging his lover to stay but ultimately getting discarded for a world of darkness. In the end it becomes his decision to leave, and there is a strength to choosing his own destiny; however, the choice still leaves uncertainty and lasting residual damage.

Beau opened up a little about the story behind the song on our night together but ever since then, every stanza I dissected seemed to have additional layers to it. There was so much beneath the surface of the story he told me. So much heartbreak.

It was perhaps even more impossible not to think about Beau Davis when I *wasn't* working on this piece. Admittedly there weren't a huge number of hours these days when I wasn't either in rehearsals or figuring out the final remaining beats after everyone else had left for the night. In those quiet fleeting moments, my thoughts flew back to the lascivious little rock star desperately scrambling to his knees for me. Beau Davis was an enigma. He was quiet and subdued in interviews. He was thoughtful and melancholy in his lyrics. And he was a kinky little spitfire in bed.

Or on his entryway floor, as the case may be.

We never actually made it to a bed that night.

Either way I couldn't figure him out, and now—more than a month later—I couldn't stop kicking myself for not asking for his number. In the moment, I had thought about it, but we both knew it was a onetime deal, and I didn't want to be the cliché groupie who didn't recognize that. Still, the worst he could have done was say no.

"Great, so we're about halfway through now. We get into a frantic bit with lots of lifts coming up here, so let's go through what we have one more time, and then we'll take five before getting into it."

Hayden and Reece nodded at my direction before resetting for their positions at the top, their limbs woven together in a lovers' embrace on the floor. I grabbed a swig from my water bottle before moving to the front of the room so I could watch from the audience perspective. Cueing up the music to the beginning of the song on my phone, I hit Play.

The opening major chord of "Galaxies" swelled through the surround-sound speakers in the studio. Knowing it was Beau's fingers on the keys creating those notes somehow made the music even more beautiful. I kept time by tapping my foot and bobbing my head, counting in the beats as the drums and the bass kicked in.

Hayden Zhang was the senior ballet student I knew I had to cast as soon as I changed the piece to feature two male dancers. His technique was flawless, and his dedication was second-to-none. The worst-kept secret at Juilliard right now was that Hayden was currently being recruited by at least three of the top national ballet companies for next season. It was going to turn into a bidding war before long, and all of my colleagues were waiting for the dramatics with our popcorn ready. Whichever company ended up winning his signature on their contract was going to be ecstatic.

At over six feet in height, Hayden was tall for a dancer, but his partnering ability was really what made him stand out on the stage. The power in his stride, in his core, and in his arms made him an enviable partner for every ballerina in the school. As such, his strength was what immediately excited me about him when I changed the piece to feature two men. I was able to add a shit-ton of lifts by casting Hayden; not many dancers would be able to consistently lift another man in the way that Reece was tossed around in this number. I couldn't have cast a more perfect person for this role if I had been given free rein of the New York City Ballet company.

On the other end of the spectrum was Reece Varga, the junior who I had wanted playing Beau's character from the very beginning. Reece was a scrappy and emotional dancer. The epitome of a performer. He was all lean muscle, and his legs were about a mile long. While his technical abilities were also above average for his group of peers, it was really his heart and the passion he poured into his characters that set him apart. Reece also had crazy aerial work and got more height on his jumps than almost any dancer I had ever seen, student or professional. In short, this duo was practically made for this performance, and creating it on them had been a choreographer's dream.

The two flew across the stage together now, hurling themselves into Beau's words, which were being sung by Carter's gravelly voice. Both men were dancing full out even though it was only rehearsal. We had been going at this for hours, and they still only knew a portion of the number, but it was like they were performing in front of a crowd of hundreds. Reece leaped onto Hayden's back, almost knocking them both over. I made a mental note to correct that, but beyond a couple of minor touch-ups, the run went pretty damn smoothly.

I pressed pause on the music when we had covered all Reece and Hayden had learned so far.

"All right guys. Looking good. Grab some water and catch your breath, but don't let your bodies cool down."

Both nodded to me as they breathed heavily.

This was going to work.

Beau

WE touched down in Germany less than twenty-four hours after I had walked into the dance studio at Juilliard and met Jamie the choreographer. The flight back to Europe was fucking depressing. Carter was barely operational, dead silent and hardly acknowledging anything or anyone. We all left him alone; he had been counting down the days until his reunion with Chase since the beginning of the tour, and being ripped apart again must be killing him. The two already had plans for Chase to fly out to meet Carter in Paris over his Christmas break, but that was almost two months away.

Our manager, Cory, was sitting a few rows ahead of me, tapping frantically on his computer for the majority of the flight. He was probably working on contracts or schedules or whatever else he did all day that kept us all organized. Ash had on his reading glasses and was working his way through a textbook, doing some serious damage with a blue highlighter. Lord knows how or why, but he had decided to take some online college classes in the middle of all of this chaos. Good on him for wanting to better himself with education, but I honestly had no idea how he was able to keep up with it all, considering our crazy schedule. Dean sat next to me, dead asleep, leaning against the window. He was wearing his big over-ear headphones that were supposed to be noise-canceling, but the classic rock he was listening to blared out for us all to hear. I had no idea how he was able to sleep with that kind of racket going on.

I spent the flight alternating between dozing and overthinking. Once Jamie left last night, it had barely been an hour before I needed to head out for the airport. I was so paranoid about sleeping through my alarms, I didn't bother trying and hoped I would be able to catch some rest on the flight. Considering how utterly exhausted I was—both from the lack of sleep and from the strenuous activities my body wasn't used to—getting my brain to turn off now was far more difficult than it should have been.

When we landed, we went straight to the hotel and I passed out as soon as my body hit the king-size mattress.

I awoke in the middle of the night, having no idea where I was or what was going on. Between the long flight, the time change, and falling asleep in the middle of the afternoon without having the forethought to set an alarm, I had completely fucked up my sleep schedule.

I lay there for a while in the dark, reflecting on the past day and the improbability of what had happened. Getting guilted into speaking to the smug students at Juilliard. Hearing my song playing down the hall when I got turned around. Meeting Jamie. Sleeping with him.

While I ultimately identified as bisexual, in general I found myself attracted to women more often than men. It took a lot for a guy to turn my head, but when someone did, I tended to fall hard and fast for him. I didn't do as many hookups with either gender as I probably could have, but I had a more difficult time doing the casual thing with guys. Not sure why, but maybe that was another reason why I had avoided hookups with men recently. I wasn't ready to get attached.

My most functional relationship had been with a woman named Laura, right when Thorns was on the verge of starting to play bigger gigs. Things had been progressing, but she was a nurse and I was a burgeoning rock musician, and our lifestyles ultimately drove a wedge between us. She was a few years older than me and was looking for someone to settle down with; I was pouring all of my energy into the band. We remained friendly, but looking back on it, breaking up had been the right decision. Several months after ending things with Laura, I started sleeping with Dylan. Maybe it was a rebound or maybe Dylan and I had been dancing around each other for a while. Either way it was an unhealthy start to an unhealthy relationship.

Being with a woman had been easier in a lot of ways. I told my dad I was bi in my senior year of high school. He basically ignored that half of me, which should have irritated me more than it did. More than it *does*. We're not close, my dad and I. Growing up I was pulled from base to base with him whenever he was relocated, which was a lot. My mom died when I was too young to remember much about her, so it was just my dad, my brother, Joe, and me. Joe and I had a stepmom at one point, but we don't talk about her anymore.

I was never the kind of kid who made friends easily, and throughout my adolescence I grew to resent my dad for moving as much as we did. Both him and my brother tend to run pretty close-minded conservative. Not only did I decide to not enlist, I didn't even end up in a macho field. I also wasn't a functioning—or quasifunctioning—alcoholic. So there was no fitting in for me in our household. Things changed a little when Thorns grew in profile, mainly because having money at least made me useful to them. Over the years my relationship with my dad and brother had gotten worse, and in general it became easier to stay away and only see them on holidays, when I had no other choice.

I dragged myself out from under the covers, my mind too geared up to allow me to sleep any longer. After throwing on some red mesh shorts and an old T-shirt, I stuffed my feet into a pair of sneakers and headed down to find the hotel's gym. While I wasn't a huge fan of working out, banging out some distance on the treadmill sometimes helped to clear my head, and I tried to do a little cardio a few times a week. Also, playing keys onstage under the scorching lights requires a surprising amount of stamina.

I found the gym abandoned, probably due to the hour. After my movement triggered the motion-sensor lights, I chose a machine that faced a window. Switching the thing on, I started at a walk and progressively increased the speed to a comfortable jog. I stared out over the city lights of Berlin, losing myself in the rhythm of my legs thumping out the miles and the white noise of the city at night. Adrenaline kicked in, and my body started to acclimate after I passed the initial hump of the exercise.

As the sweat started to slide down my chest, my thoughts returned to Jamie and how he had looked when I first saw him in the dance studio. In the bar, he'd told me how an ankle injury and the subsequent surgery had made it impossible for him to keep dancing professionally. Life had a funny way of putting some people on the exact right path, and hearing Jamie talk about choreographing sure made it seem like he had found his calling. Although I had only known him for a few hours, it was obvious he was passionate about what he did, and it was easy to assume he was someone who would fight tooth and nail until he got what he wanted. Big things were in that man's future, and I hoped one day he would get the recognition he deserved, whether or not I was ever aware of his successes.

And then there was the sex. Jamie lit up my body like nobody else I had ever met. While thoughts of pain play or serious kink made me squeamish, the secret craving to be bossed around in the bedroom had been a fantasy of mine for an embarrassing amount of time. I wasn't sure why I had felt comfortable enough with Jamie to encourage him to take control when I hadn't made the move with previous partners. It had happened so naturally it wasn't even a conversation we had. Like somehow he had recognized that desire in me and sensed exactly how far to push. The praise that had fallen from his lips while I had sucked him had ignited a spark inside me. All I'd wanted to do was please him and earn more of his positive words.

I had made a point not to consider the possibility of our tryst going beyond that one night. Knowing myself, I could too easily become enraptured by a man who fascinated me as much as Jamie did. Even though it killed me not to ask for his number before he left, it was better for him to walk away and make a clean break.

I checked the time on my phone and realized I had been running for almost an hour. My legs felt like rubber as I slowed and then stopped the treadmill. As I hit the power button to turn the machine off, I forced myself to abandon all thoughts of Jamie—eliminating him from my mind and getting back to the reality of the wonderful, grueling tour we were on.

Jamie

THE auditorium was dark around me as the familiar first chords of "Galaxies" pumped through the top-of-the-line sound system. A pool of blue light came up on Hayden and Reece, catching the shadows on both men's faces in expressions of agony and ecstasy. Sitting next to me, the stage manager, Lucas, called out a cue into his headset. More light magically appeared on the stage in time with the dancers' first movements. The lighting was beautiful and perfectly encapsulated the mood of the piece that I had been going for.

We were in day two of our technical rehearsals for the December showcase. Tomorrow everyone would be in costume for the dress rehearsal, and Friday through Sunday would be the performances. By Sunday evening, all of the months' worth of work would be over. It was the wonder and the tragedy of our world; the reward for all of the effort sometimes seemed to be so fleeting.

I noticed that the lighting wasn't quite emphasizing the legs of the dancers in the way it should be during this cue.

"Pause for a second," I said to Lucas.

"Thank you." Lucas automatically spoke into the microphone in front of him. His voice reverberated through the theater as the signal for the dancers to stop and for the audio engineer, Bria, to hold the music.

"Curt, can we get some more sidelight on their shins here? I want to capture the power of Reece's lower body as he gets ready for these leaps," I said.

Our lighting technician nodded in acknowledgment of my direction and tapped away at a few keys on his console. Light streamed in from the wings as Curt increased the intensity.

"Gorgeous," Lucas agreed. "Gonna be some wet panties in the house during this number."

I laughed out loud at his crass comment. I had worked with Lucas a couple of times over the years. He mainly took longer contracts, though sometimes our schedules lined up and he was able to coordinate accepting a few days' work on small projects for Juilliard showcases. I loved working with the guy because he was a completely competent professional when he needed to be, but he was hilarious and instantly made the stressful schedule we kept way more fun. Normally he would show up for a day or two of technical rehearsals before the performance. I knew the work I had created would come together perfectly on show day under his leadership and that he would call the lighting cues on precisely the right beat to make the whole presentation pop.

"You good, Jamie, Curt?" Lucas asked.

"Yup," Curt and I said in unison.

"Okay, guys, here we go. Bria, when you're ready," Lucas directed through the microphone.

Bria rewound the music a few seconds, and the stage came alive again with Hayden and Reece telling the story through movement. I loved the feeling of power from being in the driver's seat during tech rehearsals. There was something so glorious about completing the picture in my head and having a highly-skilled team of designers supporting my vision. Like always, the choreography was my priority and my overall forte, but the lighting, composition, and stage direction highlighted the dynamics of the dancers.

We stopped and started a handful more times over the next hour, perfecting the lighting design. Once we were all satisfied, we did one last run-through before the next group was slotted to begin.

When we were done in the theater, I followed Reece and Hayden to the wardrobe department for the final fitting of their costumes. I use the term "costumes" generously as each dancer was only wearing a tiny pair of spandex shorts. Hayden's shorts were a dark midnight blue, and Reece's were a lighter lavender color. Each had tiny threads of glitter sewn in so they would sparkle a little when the light hit them right.

My general preference for dance clothing was minimalistic—not for the sex appeal as much as to emphasize the athleticism of the dancers on the stage. These guys obviously had to keep themselves in shape to do what they do, so why not show it off? I also privately liked that the guys were wearing outfits similar to the dance shorts I'd had on when I met Beau. The look in Beau's eyes as he took in my body was burned into my memory. I don't think I had ever felt sexier in my life than when he stared at me like that.

Nobody had to know *that* reason for Hayden and Reece's attire.

"What do you want for our hair, Jamie? Any makeup?" Reece asked, running his hand through his light brown locks while staring at himself in the mirror.

"I want to keep your look natural. Put a little product in your hair, but keep it simple. Hopefully with all the movement, it'll get a bit mussed up over the course of the song. A little stubble might be good for you too. No makeup, but I have some highlight shimmer that'll go on your abs to catch the light."

Reece nodded, rubbing the back of his hand over his smooth cheek as if to imagine what it would feel like with a few days' growth.

"And Hayd, let's go a little darker for you." I moved behind where Hayden was standing facing the mirror. He played with his chin-length black hair until I indicated I was happy. "Something like that. Slick it down with gel or wax so it looks greasy. Like you haven't bothered taking care of yourself enough to wash it. Let's do some heavy eyeliner under your eyes. Think a cross between punk and haven't-slept chic. I've also picked up some real-looking temporary tattoos from the makeup department. They're all black and gray, and I'm thinking we'll make it look like you have a full sleeve down your left arm. What do you think?"

"Hell yes," Hayden replied enthusiastically.

"Super hot," Reece agreed, his eyes running up and down his dance partner's body.

Uh-oh, I thought to myself.

I had no idea whether Hayden was gay, but I knew that look, and I had no leeway for a showmance between my two dancers. It really wouldn't be appropriate for me to stop it; however, this weekend was too important to me to take any chances.

I shot Reece a warning glance, to which he had the good grace to put his palms up apologetically. Fortunately Hayden was too busy mapping out his arms for the tattoos to notice the exchange.

"All right. Go home and get some rest. The dress rehearsal tomorrow starts at 2:00 p.m., but we won't be on until—" I checked the clock on my phone. "—probably a little before three. So let's meet in the dressing room at 1:30 p.m. 'cause I wanna play with Hayden's tattoos for a bit. Great work today, guys. This is gonna be killer."

Jamie

A FEW days after the showcase, I sat at my desk at Juilliard finalizing the last of my grading for the semester when there was a knock on the doorframe. Most of the faculty and students knew I barely spent any time in my office; however, I was playing catch-up on my paperwork after being so focused on the showcase for the past few weeks.

Coleman Hale, one of my least favorite colleagues, appeared and invited himself in, sitting in the chair across from me. While Coleman had a reputation for ballet excellence at Juilliard and beyond, his tendency to get those results by any means necessary also was somewhat legendary. He was a pretentious asshole to the nth degree—at least by my calculations. Coleman walked with his nose so far in the air I was surprised he was able to breathe with the altitude. He'd hated my style of dance and everything I stood for from the moment I stepped foot in his studio during my time at the New York City Ballet. He'd *loathed* me since I went on stage in a ballet he had directed wearing a costume I had redesigned without his approval.

I always thought the detestation was mostly because that costume had received raves in the *New York Times*. That had been a blow to his ego, especially since the paper had ignored the rest of his production. Admittedly I was in the wrong in that scenario, and I would probably abhor any dancer who did the same to me, but the incident was years ago, and my costume was probably the only reason why we got mentioned in the *Times* at all.

"Mr. Griffin, I hear congratulations are in order," Coleman said. His expression was emotionless, and his words were long and drawn out.

"Why, thank you, Coleman," I said, ignoring the sarcasm in his voice and his pompous insistence upon formality. "It seemed like my dance went over quite well. I've had a lot of faculty compliments this week."

Coleman grumbled, "If one can even call that dance."

I leaned back in my chair, chewing on the end of my marking pen.

"I enjoyed your piece as well. It's always nice to see yet another performance of 'Rose Adagio.' *The Sleeping Beauty*—such a *classic*."

I was baiting him, but what the fuck ever. His piece was boring, and he knew it; he didn't even choreograph it himself, simply showed the dancers some tapes— probably still on VHS—and got them to memorize it. Coleman had been a great choreographer at one point in his career, but then at some point, he had decided to settle and get by with his past reputation alone. Perhaps it had been around the time he realized there was a younger generation of artists chomping at the bit to innovate the genre. I hoped I was never satisfied with doing the bare minimum in my own work.

"*That* was ballet! Clearly you have a hard time recognizing it." He pounded his fist on my desk like a Neanderthal, a direct contrast to the sophisticated image he endeavored to project.

"*Was* being the operative word. That *was* ballet. My piece *is* ballet. It is a living, breathing thing. Ballet is not the same as it was thirty years ago!"

The two of us remained at an impasse. We were both fired up, standing and leaning over the neutral zone of my desk. His face was flushed. My eyes were narrowed. It was the classical versus the contemporary. The past versus the future. The boomers versus the millennials. It would be equally as impossible for me to convince him that my interpretation of ballet was the correct one as for the opposite to happen. At least I believed there was somewhat of an opportunity for the two to coexist.

"Jamie! I'm so glad I caught you!" Claudia, the dean of the dance department, emerged at my door. It was difficult to tell if she had heard the raised voices or if her appearance was merely a coincidence. "Coleman, do you mind if I steal Jamie away for a moment?"

"Not at all. I was just leaving," Coleman said with a huff. He looked back at me over Claudia's shoulder with a scowl, shaking his head as he exited my office.

"Can I buy you a cup of coffee?" Claudia asked me once Coleman was gone.

"Yeah, that sounds great. I was thinking some caffeine might be in order." I glanced down at the offending paperwork, unquestionably the worst part of my job. We started walking to the coffee cart outside the main faculty office.

"Finals grading?" She asked.

I nodded. "Have I always had this many students?" I joked. "I think there are more papers than dancers in my classes."

"Well, I wouldn't imagine nonstudents decided to do some extra written exams for fun," she deadpanned.

I laughed at her quip. Though Claudia and I didn't spend a lot of time together, she was the major player on the Juilliard team who had championed my employment. She barely choreographed anymore—there were only so many hours in the day—but I remember seeing a work she did when I was younger, and she was an extraordinarily talented artist in her own right. Claudia wasn't the type to take shit or accept less than perfection, which is why I was surprised that people like Coleman were able to remain on her staff for as long as they did. There must have been politics of some sort involved.

We ordered our beverages and took up residence at one of the small tables in the foyer.

"So, Jamie. Everyone on campus is absolutely buzzing about your number at the showcase. I was there on Saturday night, and Hayden and Reece completely stole the show. It wasn't even comparable to any of the others. It's been a long damn time since I've seen anything that's made me actually want—not feel obligated—to stand and applaud at the end."

A smile spread across my cheeks. Impressing your boss was always a good feeling; impressing someone like Claudia who had sky-high standards was even more rewarding.

"Thank you," I said, trying to come off humble. "They're both strong dancers, and they did an outstanding job."

"They are. Both boys were lovely, and they did us all proud. But the concept? The song choice, the choreo. It was all *brilliant*. How did you come up with the idea?

"I had some help," I admitted, not wanting to take credit that wasn't due. I relayed the short version of the story of how I met Beau, not wanting to out him or share too much about his deeply personal song. It wasn't my story to tell beyond my interpretation of the dance piece.

Claudia listened intently, nodding and asking a few questions about some of the decisions I had made in the performance.

"I've had some interest from a videographer friend of mine," she said. "He wants to film the piece. He would keep all your choreography, maybe glitz it up a little with a couple of locations and different angles. I know that's not really your thing, but I think this could really get you some traction in your work. Maybe show it off to some other companies. And it would be good for Hayden and Reece, of course."

My eyebrows shot up in surprise. I certainly wasn't expecting something like that. Best case scenario, I thought it might be recreated at some point for a C-list professional company, or perhaps a few people would write about it in dance mags if I was really lucky. Claudia was right; I'd never had any desire to do work for film before. However this wasn't really a movie. It would be more like a promo for my choreography. Helping Hayden and Reece with some additional exposure at the start of their careers would also probably be beneficial for the two of them. I didn't see any reason why not to go ahead with Claudia's offer.

I smiled at her. "Let's do it."

Beau

THE tour pressed on. The next two months flew by. It was exhilarating. It was exhausting. Occasionally we had a day or two off between gigs when we got to explore the cities we were in. I tried to take advantage of the time when we got it as I'd never been anywhere outside the US before, but honestly some days all I wanted to do was sleep. When we were on stage, however, nothing else mattered. The venues, the crowds, the *music* were the prizes at the end of the busy days and the constant travel.

My God, they loved us.

I knew we had fans in the States, but I had *no* idea that Inevitable Thorns had gained so much popularity overseas. People living in cities where most of the population didn't even speak our language were coming out in droves to see us play. Some nights when the crowds were particularly amazing, I would turn to Carter, Dean, or Ash on stage and we would start to giggle to ourselves. It all seemed so unreal. How had a group of misfits from Nowheresville, Massachusetts possibly garnered this level of success?

The week before we paused the tour for a hiatus over the holidays, we got word that we had—for the second year in a row—received a Grammy nomination for Best Song. This year the candidate was "Lost," the single Carter and Chase had cowritten for us. We were all obviously ecstatic, but Carter himself was a hilarious fucking mess. He must have blubbered on the phone with Chase for two hours that day. It was a big deal—don't get me wrong—it was just too funny how much of a sap Cart became around his man.

After that bit of excitement, the inevitable sinking feeling hit. The countdown was on until I would fly to my dad's place in Missouri to spend Christmas with him and my brother. I didn't particularly want to, but I hadn't seen them in almost two years, and I couldn't come up with an excuse not to go. So we finished the last set of shows in Paris, dropped off Carter at the arrivals gate where Chase's flight was due to land at any moment, and the rest of us headed to the other end of the airport to fly back to the States for a few weeks.

Culture shock.

That was the best way to put it.

Going from being a successful musician performing in front of thousands of screaming fans every night to being met at the airport in Johnson County, Missouri, by my older brother in his crappy, rusted-out pickup truck was an enormous letdown. It wasn't even like I was returning home and could fuck off to see buddies

I went to school with. My dad had been transferred several times since I lived with him, so this place held no sentimental value to me at all. Life went from the highest high to the lowest low in the span of twenty-four hours.

Dad had been hurt on the job a few years back—not even in a war zone but in a minor car accident on the base. I'm almost positive that his injury wasn't as bad as he claimed, as they denied him long-term disability, but now he's stuck at a desk job he hates. He was never a warm and fuzzy kind of parent growing up, but a layer of bitterness had crept in now that was never there before.

After twenty minutes of awkward silence in the truck, we pulled up at the off-base house my dad and brother lived in. My brother Joe was a civilian contractor on the base. Even when we were growing up, we had little in common. Joe took after my dad—a man's man. Sunday nights were spent screaming themselves hoarse at whatever football game was on TV. They started going to the gun range together every Saturday as soon as Joe was old enough. And these days, Fridays were reserved for getting hammered at the local Irish pub. They were like two peas in a pod, and I was the awkward eggplant nobody quite knew what to do with.

The whole place reeked of booze and stale air when I walked in, quickly discovering the reason my father hadn't bothered to pick me up from the airport: he was passed out on the couch with a bottle of vodka still precariously clutched in his hand. I rolled my eyes. Merry Christmas to me.

As I wheeled my suitcase into my brother's room, I took in the scene. The two of them at least had the forethought to set out a single air mattress for me on the floor. It was even in a prime location—directly under a poster of an almost-naked starlet who looked barely old enough to be legal. Score. A neon beer sign blinked obnoxiously at me from above Joe's unmade bed, what looked like the sole lighting fixture in the room. I sighed deeply and reminded myself that they were family and this was only for a few weeks.

"Hey, bro, can you spot me fifty bucks?" Joe asked, coming up behind me from the living room.

"Hmm?" I said absently before pulling out my wallet from my back pocket automatically. I handed Joe a bill.

"Cool. Going out for groceries. Be back in a bit."

My stomach growled at the mention of food. Once I heard the engine of Joe's truck putter down the driveway, I went into the kitchen to see if I could find a snack. I opened the fridge and almost recoiled at the smell. A six-pack of beer and two paper to-go boxes greeted me, as well as a few packets of various sauces, and one very brown apple. I sniffed the takeout cartons cautiously before covering my mouth to prevent retching.

They had been in there for *a while.*

Locating the overflowing garbage can under the sink, I threw the apple and what was once Chinese food inside before tying up the bag and trekking the whole thing outside to the dumpster.

Returning to the kitchen, I sorted through the cupboards one by one looking for anything else that was edible. I found some plates, a few cups, a pot or two. Some salt, pepper, and instant coffee. A container with bottles of pain pills and other medication. A pantry overflowing with empties. An expired half-full box of crackers.

My stomach was sour from the way these two were living. They both had steady paychecks, and the housing was subsidized by the base. I sent some cash to them every month and almost always gave them more when they asked. Where the fuck was the money going?

A hiccup sounded from the other room, followed by the groan of springs.

"Fuckin' goddamn piece-of-shit couch," my dad slurred. He kicked the leg of the sofa when he stood up, which caused him to stumble and spill the vodka he still held.

"Fuck!" he screamed at the now-empty bottle and threw it clean across the room. It hit the wall and shattered into pieces.

"Dad! What the fuck are you doing?" I yelled from the kitchen.

I couldn't believe all this bullshit. It was so much worse than it used to be, and I now understood exactly why there was no money for groceries in the house. I was honestly terrified to get closer. My dad had never turned to physical violence against me when I was younger, but this version of him was someone I didn't know at all.

"Well if it ain't Mr. Celebrity. Ran out o' money so he comes crrrrawling back," he said.

"I didn't run out of money, Dad. We're on break for Christmas, and I'm visiting. My band is on tour, remember?"

"Oh, yeah. I 'member now. With that singer. The queer." His face contorted into an angry grimace, and he lost his footing again and fell back onto the couch.

Before I could say anything else, the front door opened, and Joe walked through. He had a brown paper bag from the liquor store, which looked full, and one of those rotisserie chickens from the market.

"I thought you were buying groceries?"

Joe held up the chicken by way of explanation, clearly either not remembering—or not caring—that I had been a vegetarian since I was twelve. Something in me snapped as I stared at the pathetic parcels my money had gone toward. I didn't particularly want to be here in the first place, and now seeing how things had become and the lack of any effort whatsoever, I couldn't stand the thought of three weeks in this house with their drinking and their hate.

Spending the night on the steadily-deflating air mattress—listening to my brother's foghorn snores and my own rumbling stomach—I allowed myself to think about Jamie for the first time in months. His laugh, the way he moved on the dance floor. How impossibly good it felt to kiss him. His moans. His praise. I *missed* him. I barely knew him, but I missed him. Was that even possible? Finally sometime late in the night, I fell asleep with his gorgeous face on my mind and a smile on my lips.

I snuck out of the house early the next morning with my suitcase, leaving a note on the counter that I would *not* be staying for Christmas.

Jamie

MY phone lit up on my nightstand, pulling me from the last fragments of sleep. Grumbling, I cursed whichever of my friends was texting me so early on my day off. I stretched my arms and then picked up my phone to see who I needed to kill.

Whoa.

I had a screenful of notifications from Twitter, Instagram, Facebook, YouTube, and every other platform of social media you could name. There were also fifty-seven missed phone calls and over 200 unread text messages.

Before I went to bed the previous night, I had seen that Karim, Claudia's videographer friend, had uploaded the final "Galaxies" video we'd made. I was thrilled with the finished product he had created, and I was glad that a few of my dance friends who couldn't make the Juilliard showcase would get to see it.

What I hadn't expected was to wake up with the video hitting 1.3 million views overnight. Holy shit. I was getting notifications from major pop-culture dance celebrities who had shared it. I had tens of thousands of new followers on my personal accounts. We were well on our way to going viral. There were *memes*, for Christ's sake!

Against my better judgment, I scrolled through the comments section on YouTube to see what people were saying. The comments were overwhelmingly positive, with a few obvious crude and cruel remarks thrown in for balance. People were talking about Hayden and Reece's obvious connection, along with their skills and attractive looks. They were talking about the story, about my choreography. There were a couple of questions raised regarding the song itself; it was not a particularly well-known song in Thorns's catalog, so it didn't get a huge amount of radio play or discussion in interviews. As I had also wrongly assumed due to the lack of pronouns in the song, there was some speculation about whether it was actually intended to be about two guys. Of those making that conjecture, most assumed it was a song Carter had written. They were wondering if that meant there were problems between Carter and Chase, after Carter's very public declaration at last year's *Grammys*. I felt pretty badly about that, even though those comments were a little bit of a stretch.

Fortunately I hadn't read any comments suggesting it was Beau who had written "Galaxies" or that it was somehow his story. Most listeners don't bother to check liner notes these days, so it wasn't a surprise that hardly anyone seemed to know he wrote the song. Beau was a private person and while I didn't think he was exactly closeted, he wasn't really out publicly either. I would have felt horrible if my piece had outed him without his permission. Not that I would have ever guessed all this chaos would have erupted from our little video. I chuckled to myself, remembering that last night I was merely excited to show the number to a few dance friends and family members.

I glanced to the side of my screen and saw the massive list of related videos. Concert footage, professional music videos, and fan tributes to the Thorns were now somehow comparable to my little dance film. One of the thumbnails in particular caught my eye. It was a close-up on Beau's smiling face in the sun—looking natural and candid. I ran my fingers over his lovely features, wishing I could feel his soft skin instead of the cold glass. When I clicked on the video, Beau's laugh erupted through my speakers, filling the quiet room. His exuberance lit me up, and I grinned along with him.

The short clip was from the Thorns official channel and featured behind-the-scenes footage of a photoshoot they had done a few months ago for *Rolling Stone* magazine. The four of them were on a pool deck, having a fantastic time joking and goofing off for the cameras. It certainly didn't hurt that Beau was only wearing a small pair of swim trunks, but his captivating joyfulness was what did me in.

I longed to be the focus of that smile again.

Would Beau somehow see the video for the "Galaxies" dance? And if so, would he like it? Should I try to reach out and show it to him? I desperately hoped he would approve of what I had created if he ever saw the finished product.

My phone started to ring, bringing me out of my reverie. I saw Hayden's name flash across my call display, and I swiped to answer him.

"Ho-ly shit," I said by way of greeting.

"What the crap happened?" Hayden's voice responded through the speaker, slightly panicky. "We… I… went to bed last night and—"

"—and the entire world saw you dance," I cut him off, refraining from calling him out on his slip.

"I don't know what to do about this." Hayden laughed nervously.

"Me neither. I guess we see what happens?"

"Oh my God, babe! Ellen just shared it!" someone who sounded unsurprisingly like Reece squealed in the background of Hayden's call.

"Jamie, I gotta go. Give me a call when you figure out what happens next!" Hayden quickly cut off the phone.

I rolled my eyes at the pair of them for their lack of subtlety. At least they had waited until after the showcase.

THE next week was absolute madness. Along with visiting my family for a few days and running around between holiday obligations, I got calls from every major dance company in the country. Some begged me to come and be a guest choreographer. Others tried to convince me to persuade Hayden, Reece, or both to join up with them. Some simply wanted to congratulate me. My dad had shared the video with literally everyone he knew, which was incredible except whenever I left his house one of his friends or neighbors wanted to have an hour-long conversation.

I fielded messages from podcasts, YouTubers, and late-night shows. I even got a strange message from someone claiming to be a producer of the *Grammy Awards*. It was hard to tell what was real and what was fake anymore. And through it all, the counts on the video just kept climbing.

Beau

ONE of the few luxuries I purchased for myself when Thorns started making significant money was a small oceanfront cabin in Bar Harbor, Maine. It was a beautiful coastal town. I had mostly chosen the location because it was one of the few states I had never lived in before. There were no unpleasant memories from my family, and a deep sense of peace always filled me when I spent time there. When I left the horror that was my dad's house, my thumbs seemed to automatically book my flight to Maine without my even thinking about it. I had almost three whole weeks on my own until I rejoined the band in Los Angeles for the *Grammys* before we all headed back to Europe to continue the tour. Until then I had nowhere to go, no expectations to meet, and nobody to respond to.

After renting an SUV at the airport, I settled in for the drive to Bar Harbor. Though I didn't drive much these days, it all came back to me quickly enough when I was behind the wheel, and before long I was singing with the radio, thoroughly enjoying myself. I stopped at the grocery store and loaded my cart with as much vegetarian food as I desired without feeling the least bit guilty about the price or the volume of the items. It was my own personal "fuck you" to my brother.

I breathed a sigh of relief when I unlocked the door to my cottage. It smelled musty and stale inside, so I opened the windows to let in the December air, despite how cold it was. The house was secluded, high on a cliff overlooking the crashing waves of the unsettled ocean below. It was small, relatively modest, and decorated comfortably. Most importantly there wasn't one broken vodka bottle or trashy beer sign in sight. After putting some dressing on a bagged salad I'd bought at the store, I sat down in the breakfast nook to eat my lunch and decompress.

Some people may view spending Christmas alone as being depressing. It certainly didn't feel that way to me. I was peopled-out from the tour, and time alone was exactly what I needed, regardless of the season. Two days after I arrived at the cottage, I celebrated Christmas by playing my keyboard all day: a private concert for the wood-burning fireplace and the churning sea. I chatted with Carter briefly—giving him the CliffsNotes version of what had happened—and texted the rest of the band before shutting off my phone again.

I spent the following weeks recharging my batteries. I walked along the rocky beach. I fooled around on my keyboard. I read.

As much as I tried not to think about Jamie, sometimes I indulged myself. I wondered how he was. What he was doing for the holidays. What had happened with the dance he was working on to "Galaxies." The number was still raw and experimental when I saw him by himself in the studio. Although I had no knowledge of ballet whatsoever, I knew what he was creating was something special, regardless of the gender of the dancers he would ultimately decide to cast.

I thought about the sex we had. How it awoke something inside of me that was a little scary but had always been there. I longed for Jamie's touch. For his approval. For him to get rough with me. To actually have time to explore things between us properly. I knew I was playing a dangerous game, close to repeating past mistakes and obsessing over someone I could never have. But I couldn't seem to stop myself. That was the only downside to having so much time to myself.

I considered turning on my phone and using Grindr or Tinder to find a hookup, maybe try to decode if someone else's bossiness would turn me on in the same way, or if it was a Jamie-specific kink. It wasn't until I thought about uploading a profile picture that I realized how mortifying it would be if a fan found me on the app. Even if I chose to use a shot of my body instead of my face—like so many men and women on these sites elect to do—the goal was to end up actually meeting someone in person. So I abandoned that idea pretty quickly.

At least not wanting to be recognized was the excuse I gave myself.

When I was in bed at night—horny and aching for release—it was only ever Jamie who I thought about.

His name was always the one that fell from my lips as I tumbled over the ledge.

At the end of three weeks, I packed my things and locked up the cottage that had been my sanctuary. For the first time in a long while, I felt rested. Coming out to Maine was exactly what I'd needed.

This year we were performing at the *Grammys* in addition to being nominated, which added another level of stress to the whole thing. The good news was we got a rehearsal on stage the day before the live event, and because Thorns hadn't played together in almost a month, we were sure going to need it. Driving down the freeway, I headed toward the airport with no idea what would hit me once I got to LA.

Jamie

HOW has this become my life? I wondered for the
thousandth time as I lay in the luxurious sheets of the
Ritz-Carlton hotel in downtown Los Angeles. In less
than an hour, I would be inside the Staples Center in
rehearsals for the freaking *Grammy Awards*.

Our little dance video had continued to pick up
steam over the past few weeks. It seemed every day
a different celebrity would reach out or we would hit
a new milestone for the number of views. We were
somewhere over nine million now. It was insane. I
had no idea why the video had caused such bedlam.
I guessed it simply spoke to people. The petty side of
me wanted to yell "I told you so!" in Coleman Hale's
hollow face, but I deftly refrained.

I had tried to reach out to Beau a couple of times through private messages on his socials. At first I wanted to make sure he didn't feel taken advantage of or outed by me—even though I had yet to read any comments linking the content of my piece to Beau's personal life and sexual identity. Then, after I had gotten the call that the producers wanted to take advantage of the video's hype and have Reece and Hayden dance live with the band at the *Grammys*, I had hoped to be able to warn Beau and make sure he didn't have a problem with me being there on his big night. But he hadn't responded either time, so there wasn't much else I could do. Beau wasn't very active on social media to begin with; I had no idea if he truly hadn't received my messages or if he was choosing to ignore them. Maybe he didn't even handle his accounts himself. Wasn't that something that famous people sometimes had staff for?

I met Hayden and Reece in the lobby of the hotel. Between the three of us, we wheeled suitcases filled with all of our gear down the street. The two of them were buzzing with excitement—and nerves—as we showed our IDs and gained access to the facility. As the authority figure, I at least tried to be cool about the whole thing. The performance itself would be a little different from the showcase at Juilliard. I knew we didn't have much depth on the stage as the band would be behind the dancers, and the moody lighting would be brighter to translate well on camera. We agreed we would work with whatever happened; it was simply too big an opportunity to be picky about.

"Oh my fuck," Reece said, eyes wide, as we were shuffled onto the stage by a production assistant.

The arena was *huge*. Stagehands bustled around from every corner, working on the set, the lighting, the speakers in preparation for the big show. Camera crews huddled in various pockets, checking and rechecking their instructions. Assistants talked briskly into radios and made frantic notes on their clipboards. Front-of-house staff taped names to the seats of the A-list celebrities who would be in attendance. I had danced for some relatively large crowds before in professional settings, but I had *never* experienced anything anywhere near this scale.

"Okay Jamie, Hayden, Reece, I'll take you to your dressing room. You have about an hour to get ready before we'll need you. Someone will call you over the intercom, and you'll come back here. In the show tomorrow, "Galaxies" will be the final song in Thorns's set, but we're going to do it first today because it's the most complicated. Cool?" the PA said in a succinct tone.

We nodded, all three of us entirely overwhelmed by the situation.

Beau

PULLING off my sunglasses, I walked out of the bright sunlight and into the stage entrance of the Staples Center. I made small talk with the guard as he verified my ID and checked me in. Immediately one of the assistants appeared to take me to the stage, where the rest of the band was setting up.

"I'm sorry, do we know you? This is a closed rehearsal," Carter greeted me with a wide grin and a hug. "Good to see you're still alive, man. You could have at least texted once or twice."

"Hey, I called you on Christmas," I said, shoving him playfully on the arm for talking shit.

"You doing okay with the family stuff?" Carter's voice got serious, keeping his tone low and looking around to make sure nobody overheard.

I appreciated his concern and how he understood that I didn't want the whole world hearing my drama.

"Yeah, it's fine. Haven't talked to them, but I'm all right. I just snapped, ya know? Like, I made the effort to come all that way and he couldn't even stay sober long enough to meet me at the airport." I ran my fingers through my hair.

Carter nodded empathetically. "Good for you, though. You've put up with way too much of his bullshit over the years."

I made a sound of agreement, which turned into an embarrassing squeal as Dean chose that moment to jump on my back and wrap his legs around my waist.

"What the fuck, man. Get off!" I shook myself to try to detach our bass player as Carter howled with laughter. Fucker probably saw Dean behind me the whole time.

"But I misssssed you!" Dean clung to me tighter and stuck a disgusting, wet kiss on the back of my neck.

"Blegh," I complained loudly as I felt my legs start to give with the extra weight. I refused to fall to the ground, though, knowing from experience that would give Dean an opening to start a dogpile on me. At least we were maintaining our reputation of professionalism around the biggest players in the business.

As I was spinning in every direction trying to shake our stubborn bassist, I caught a flash of a familiar smile off to my right.

No.

There was no way.

My mind and my body froze simultaneously. I unceremoniously dumped Dean off my back, not even hearing his woeful protest. Still not believing my eyes, I took one step and then another until I was standing immediately in front of the man who had been on my mind for the last three months.

"Hey, rock star," Jamie said quietly. His smile was cocky, but he pushed his hands into the pockets of his lilac-colored hoodie as if unsure what to do with them.

I was aware that all the members of my band were staring at us questioningly, but I couldn't bring myself to care.

"What are you doing here?" I asked reverently, terrified that if I actually spoke to him, he would turn into a mirage and fade into the abyss before my eyes.

"Dancing. Well, they are." He let out a beautiful awkward laugh and gestured to two guys standing close to him. The two men in question were stretching in what looked like impossible positions. One, possibly of Asian heritage, had dark hair and a sleeve of tattoos. The other man was shorter and had a disarray of caramel locks. They were both wearing nothing but tiny little shorts almost identical, apart from their color, to the pair Jamie wore on the day we met.

"I tried to warn you," Jamie continued. "I wasn't sure if you got my messages or if you didn't want to see me."

"Of course I want to see you. I—"

"Oh, good. You've met," our manager Cory, Core for short, said as he stepped between Jamie and me, cutting off our conversation.

I flinched a little. Core obviously had no idea about my past encounter with Jamie and that we had actually "met" a few months ago, but that was irrelevant at the moment. I still had absolutely no idea what was going on and it sounded like there wouldn't be much time for an explanation. Ash was already hitting each of his drums in a slow, repetitive way, indicating the first step of sound check had begun.

"Beau, Cory, we're gonna need you in a second here," one of the sound technicians called to us from the wings.

"Sorry, what's going on?" I asked Core, helplessly confused.

"I sent you like five emails; didn't you check them?" Cory asked. I shook my head, clearly I had missed something important when I'd neglected the outside world over the break.

"These are the guys from that video. The one of them dancing to "Galaxies" that went viral? Producers wanted to capitalize on the hype and get them to perform live with you tomorrow. The rest of the band was into the idea. Hope you're cool with it?"

I blinked rapidly, piecing together what Cory had told me and the dance number Jamie had been working on when we first met.

Fuck. It must have turned out crazy good to catch the attention of not only the dance world but the mass market and the music industry.

"Yeah. Yeah, cool." I nodded, still trying to fully process what was happening. I didn't miss the smile and exhale from Jamie when I confirmed my approval.

"Beau?" Carter called out to me from his position at the center microphone stand. He gestured with his fingers to my keyboard and raised his eyebrows as if to make sure everything was good.

"Sorry, I'm ready," I said over my shoulder to Carter and took a step back toward where the band was set up.

Beau

"**YOU** okay?" Carter asked me quietly, his mouth strategically away from his live microphone as I walked by him to take my position.

"Yeah, I'm good."

"You had no idea about any of this, did you?" Carter's eyes sparkled with humor.

"Nope. My own damn fault for turning off my phone for weeks on end." I attempted to play it off with a shrug.

"They're gonna rock it. Watch the video tonight if you get a chance. Chase showed it to me a couple weeks ago, and it's pretty insane."

"When you two are done with your little chitchat, we're all waiting around here ready to do a fucking show!" Cory hollered from the wings.

Carter rolled his eyes at Cory being a drama queen, and I made myself comfortable behind the keys. I gave Cory and Carter the thumbs-up.

The overhead fluorescents in the arena snapped off so only the theatrical stage lights remained illuminating the stage. The two dancers assumed their positions in some sort of intimate embrace. I took an audible breath—the universal signal prior to the beginning notes of a song—and pressed my hands down on the smooth keys.

When I play piano, my mind often does this thing where the rest of the world fades away and all that's left is the music. Today, on the eve of one of the biggest performances of my career, the opposite happened. I was overrun with a barrage of disjointed thoughts, relentlessly hammering into me like an unending freight train. Thank God I had played this song so often that my muscle memory took over and my fingers flew over the keys on their own accord, but it was still unsettling to be so distracted.

I thought about Dylan: the drugs, the instability, the loneliness. It was a song I had written about him, after all. A beautiful and fucked-up form of therapy. I thought about my dad and Joe, the self-destructive cycle they were caught in without even realizing it. I thought about my mom and wondered how things might have been different if the cancer had been caught earlier. I thought about my band brothers, glancing at each one in turn as they poured their hearts out into my pain. Without Dean, Ash, and Carter, I literally had no idea where I would be right now. I was infinitely grateful for them all and the lives we had built together.

My focus shifted to the two men in front of me, physically interpreting this song that meant so much.

I recognized some of the sequences from staring at Jamie in the studio on that day, which now seemed so long ago. The two dancers were *gorgeous* together. Not just in their movements but in their emotions and how they felt the rhythm of the song. Ballet was a medium I had always considered to be way above my level of sophistication, yet nothing about this felt ostentatious. This was the dance equivalent to me choosing to play the keyboard over the piano; it was like they were taking something that maybe felt a little stuffy and disingenuous and creating their own set of rules.

Both men were exceedingly talented and a pleasure to watch. However it was their invisible third partner— the apex of the triangle—who captivated me the most. I risked looking over to where he was seated in the auditorium.

Jamie.

He caught my gaze, and my breath stalled in my chest. I forced myself to exhale, coerced my fingers to keep playing the song. Even from here I could see the intensity of his eyes staring at me. They made me feel excitement and hope. They made me feel talented and wanted. They made me feel *lust*. I could barely focus on anything else. Jamie's eyes burned into me— burned deep into my soul—and compelled me to offer him anything he desired. They were penetrating eyes. Dangerous eyes.

I wanted nothing more than to give in.

Jamie

SITTING next to the lighting designer and the stage manager, I couldn't help but liken the situation to when I sat with Lucas and Curt as we prepared for the Juilliard showcase. The difference, of course, was the heated gaze of the keyboardist, locked on me every time I glanced his way. Which was admittedly a whole lot.

Fortunately the designer didn't require much direction, and there wasn't a lot for me to do other than eye-fuck Beau. I watched Hayden and Reece do their thing—and *kill it*, I might add—but mostly I sat back and enjoyed the experience.

Clearly Beau'd had no idea we were involved in the performance before today. He certainly didn't seem upset about it from the way he'd reacted when he saw me, though admittedly I didn't know him well enough to make any concrete assumptions. Hell, I had known we would see each other this afternoon, and it still somehow caught me off guard when we ended up face-to-face. Here was a man who had been on my mind—consciously or subconsciously—for months. I had never expected to see him again, yet somehow, through the craziest of circumstances, here we were. More than anything I needed to find a way to get him alone and talk to him about what had happened. I wanted to make sure he knew that I hadn't planned or intended any of this when we met and that I was more surprised than anyone by the success our video had garnered.

My attention kept floating back to him. It was impossible not to look. He was so damn handsome up there under the lights. His fingers floated effortlessly over the keys in a display of passion and strength. It was like part of his soul was released with every chord, a small piece of his burden stripped away. I had never seen Inevitable Thorns perform live before, so I was curious if Beau played like that in every song, or just the ones he wrote. The lyrics in this one felt so personal.

My concentration got wrenched away from the keyboardist when out of nowhere, Hayden appeared to slip on the stage. He caught himself before falling too hard, but he went down on his wrist at what looked like a painful angle. I rushed up the side stairs as the band cut off the music. Reece was already beside Hayd, making sure he was okay. I kneeled down and took Hayden's arm in my own, pressing and feeling to assess for injury.

"I'm fine," Hayden said.

He stretched out the limb in question and rolled his wrist once or twice. A mild grimace lined his face.

"Can we get some ice, please?" I asked one of the assistants who was standing to the side of the stage. She ran away diligently to track down a cold compress.

"I'm fine," Hayden repeated. "I'll put some ice on it, but it's nothing. I'm used to doing that landing on Marley, and I didn't adjust for that."

Last week I had asked Hayden and Reece if they had wanted me to request the vinyl, nonslip floor for their performance. The Marley floor would take time to install and would only be relevant for their lone dance number. Hayd and Reece had assured me it was unnecessary. I now chastised myself for my own stupidity, feeling responsible for not insisting on it. Fortunately it didn't seem like Hayden was badly injured, so I took it as a lesson and tried to shake the feeling of guilt.

The assistant returned with an ice pack.

"So we're about ten minutes away from the scheduled meal break," she said. "Do you want to break early and give Hayden a chance to rest? We can run it one more time when we're back before we really need to move on to the rest of Thorns's set."

She was directing her words at Cory, knowing he was ultimately the one responsible for making that decision for the band. We were on their schedule today; it was so amazing to be here and be included, but the performance was ultimately about the Thorns.

"Yup, works for us." Cory nodded. "Guys, lunch!"

"Go. Sit in the dressing room and rest," I directed Hayden. "Keep the ice on it for at least fifteen minutes, and don't even think about doing anything strenuous."

I knew my words were harsher than usual as soon as they came out of my mouth, but Hayden had scared the crap out of me, and I wasn't taking any chances.

Reece winked at me as the two of them stood up, silently letting me know he had it covered.

"Is he okay?" Beau's voice asked from much closer than I expected. I turned to look at him. His eyebrows were furrowed with concern.

"Yeah," I said, letting out a deep breath. "Stuff like that happens pretty often. He'll be fine. Just scared me, ya know? I should've said something about the floor."

"It's not your fault," Beau said gently. He reached out tentatively and touched the back of my hand.

The simple brush of his fingers felt like a thousand watts of electricity. It was a match to a forest full of dry kindling. It was the first drops of rain after a drought. It was *everything*. The hairs on my arms prickled. His eyes smoldered. My blood was on fire. I gestured subtly with my head for him to follow me.

He bit his lower lip and nodded.

Beau

I GLANCED around the abandoned backstage hallway one last time before following Jamie into the small single-occupancy washroom. We probably could have gone to my dressing room, or even back to the hotel next door, but the thought of delaying this by even a few extra seconds was not an option.

Thinking straight was impossible. I couldn't process anything besides wanting him. As soon as the door clicked shut behind us, he turned around to face me, his expression hard and predatory. I moaned desperately with anticipation as he gripped my face with both hands and took my mouth. Jamie held me forcefully and directed me where he wanted me. I opened for him eagerly. The kiss was exactly like I remembered and everything I needed. Frantic. Clawing. His tongue plunged deeply, energetically stroking and tasting me everywhere at once. All of the other busy thoughts in my head subsided, and all that existed was him.

The bathroom counter dug into my lower back as he crowded me against it. Clutching the sides of the sink, I tried to find purchase. Jamie helped me scramble up and sit on the ledge. I spread my knees a little so he could stand between them. He groaned when I wrapped my legs around him, pulling him tight and pressing our cocks together. Jamie rubbed his groin against mine, creating the most mind-blowing friction. His nimble fingers reached for my belt, unbuckling it quickly. He struggled for a moment with the complicated button fly on my jeans.

"Why the fuck would you wear these?" he asked.

"Didn't know… didn't know you were gonna be here," I panted.

Jamie kissed me hard, evidently liking my answer.

"That's why I wore these." He winked at me with a smile.

Stretching the elastic waistband, he pulled the cock I had been fantasizing about for months out of his black Lycra pants as I shimmied my jeans down over my hips.

He took another half step closer to me and fisted both of our dicks together. My whole body shuddered. Watching his silky-smooth, fiery-hot, granite-hard length moving in a tantric rhythm against my own was one of the hottest things I had ever seen. I tried to move my hips to do some of the work, but between my precarious perch on the counter and my pants barely giving any purchase, there wasn't much I could contribute. When I tried to grasp for his shirt to drag him closer, Jamie reached for both of my wrists with his left hand.

"Nuh-uh," he said, clucking his tongue and shooting me a filthy smile.

He pinned my hands up over my head against the mirror, crossing my wrists and holding them in place. My pulse skyrocketed. Jamie kept up the punishing pace of his strokes. Even with our precome mixing and helping to glide the way, it was still a little rough. With my arms incapacitated, I was powerless to do more than take the pleasure he gave me. I knew that if I really wanted to, I could get away, but this ethereal feeling of calm washed over me. It was exactly the same as the previous time with Jamie, when he had used my mouth. I made a carnal sound deep in my throat as he brushed over the head of my leaking cock.

His fingertips dug tighter into my wrists as his body grew more tense. Jamie's forearms were a work of art, and the straining and pumping were showing off his corded muscles in all their glory.

"Oh God," I moaned.

His eyes fluttered closed, and his mouth rested in an O-shape. It was a look of utter hedonism that would be permanently etched in my mind. The sounds of flesh meeting flesh grew in urgency as I rapidly hurdled toward the point of no return. I struggled against my restraints as the tension in my body built. Though I recognized we both needed something to push us over the edge, I wasn't thinking clearly enough to realize what that was.

Like a light coming on, I suddenly figured it out.

"Please," I said, barely more than a desperate breath.

Jamie's eyes flew open and met mine. The heat in his was palpable at my begging word. He groaned loudly enough that anyone passing by the bathroom would have overheard.

"Come," he ordered.

It was like a dam had broken. That permission was what my body had been waiting for. The tingling in my spine grew until the overwhelming feeling of ecstasy consumed my entire being. My brain short-circuited as my cock erupted and spilled over. Jamie spasmed against me—almost simultaneously since we'd been brought to the brink within seconds of each other. It was a trip to feel so in sync. I bit into my lower lip to prevent myself from yelling out. Some people seemed to take pleasure from forcing themselves to stay silent, but that certainly didn't describe me. I wanted to fucking scream.

Eventually the shocks waned, and a sense of serene euphoria overcame me. My body relaxed in a way that it never seemed to when it was me and my hand. Jamie smiled tranquilly at me, and I returned the expression. He kissed my lower lip softly—once, twice—before pressing our foreheads together.

"We should probably get back," he said.

I nodded in agreement. After taking another moment to calm my racing pulse, I slid down from the counter. Jamie washed our combined releases off his hands before handing me some wet paper towels to clean up the best I could.

"You know," he said conversationally, "that's the second time we've done that, and I still haven't seen you naked."

I chuckled lightly as I buttoned my fly.

"Guess we'll have to do this in a proper bed next time." I wiggled my eyebrows exaggeratedly.

"The horror! Taking my time with you? Kissing every inch of your body? Bringing you to the edge over and over before I finally let you come? I guess I might be able to work with that."

My body seemed unable to decide between being amused and being helplessly turned on again.

"You're a dork," I finally told him with a laugh.

He dabbed one last spot of come from my shirt before kissing the side of my mouth sweetly.

"Maybe. But you want it too."

I didn't even bother trying to deny it.

Jamie

BEAU left the washroom first, and I stayed in there for a minute or two with a smile etched on my lips. The second time with my little rock star was as explosive as the first, and the implication that there would be a third time lit me up to my core. I knew the likelihood of ever seeing him again after tomorrow was low. But I'd also thought that the first time. Maybe at least now I could justify asking for his number and us becoming friends or something.

Glancing at the time on my phone, I noted I had about fifteen minutes before needing to be back on stage. I scanned the hall and walked out of the bathroom when the coast was clear. As I rounded the corner, I saw Beau talking to the lead stagehand, so I ducked into the greenroom before he noticed me. There was no way I could keep a straight face around him right now, and the stagehand would surely suspect something was up. Not that it really mattered what he thought, but still....

Fortunately there was food left out for us in the greenroom, and I was able to grab a quick sandwich on my way to check in with Hayden about his injury. I stuck my nose into his and Reece's shared dressing room, hoping I didn't smell like sex.

Hayden was stretching out his quads, getting himself warmed up to go back on stage.

"Where'd you get off to?" Reece asked, looking up from his phone.

I mentally chuckled at how unintentionally accurate Reece's phrasing was. "Just had some stuff to take care of."

Reece looked like he was going to ask me more questions but then thought better of it.

"How's your wrist, Hayd?" I asked.

"It's fine. Doesn't hurt," Hayden said. "I'll ice it again tonight to be safe, but it's not anything serious."

"Good."

I ate the last bite of my sandwich and threw the wrapping in the garbage. The guys and I shot the shit for a few minutes before the speaker in the ceiling came to life, calling us back to finish rehearsal.

I held the door open for Hayden and Reece so they could walk in front of me. As we reentered the stage, I noticed a number of stagehands down on their knees with big rolls of black tape. They were almost finished installing a Marley dance floor.

Beau and his bandmates were standing in a circle next to the drum kit, well back from the working technicians. Somehow I knew immediately that this was what Beau had been arranging with the lead stagehand in the hallway. My stomach gave a funny lurch, overwhelmingly touched by Beau's kind gesture. While the floor was for the dancers, Beau had organized it because of me. He understood how concerned I was about Hayden and Reece's safety and how guilty I felt for Hayden's fall.

It was a simple thing he had done—requesting a relatively easy fix because of a safety concern—and with Beau's status it was no surprise the technicians were taking care of it right away. But the thought and care of the gesture wasn't something I would expect from a guy I had casually hooked up with.

From across the room, I looked up through my lashes at Beau, who met my gaze despite being surrounded by the Thorns. Smiling, I mouthed "Thank you," which didn't feel like nearly enough. He winked at me—setting my pulse on fire—before returning to the conversation with his friends.

We roared through the number quickly after that. The band sounded unbelievable when they were playing full out, and Reece and Hayden took it to another level in the final rehearsal. Even though I hadn't really picked up on it before, it was evident both of them were more confident with the Marley under their feet. Their jumps were higher and their landings more controlled. Hayden didn't seem to be favoring his wrist in any way, so I was happy we seemed to be in the clear with that.

Even though I tended to choreograph to nontraditional ballet music, I had never worked with a live band before. The Thorns, Reece, and Hayden were *fire* together. I had no idea how it worked—rock music and ballet—but the symbiosis was seamless, and the whole piece gelled beautifully.

Once the higher-ups were satisfied, I gathered my things, and the dancers and I got ready to leave for the day. On my way toward the exit, I purposely planned my path to take me past Beau's keyboard.

"Room 1401," I said out of the corner of my mouth, timing my words perfectly to align with my steps so only he could hear me.

Beau nodded almost imperceptibly.

Beau

WHEN we finished sound check, Carter and I decided to go out and grab dinner. It wasn't often anymore that the two of us got to spend time one-on-one. Carter was always full-on when he was with the band, but these days he usually spent his downtime skyping with Chase. It was a change in the dynamic of the band, but we were all so sick of each other after our first national tour last year that maybe it was good for our longevity that we weren't spending every waking hour together.

Chase was in the middle of his senior year at Juilliard, studying music composition. While he was able to come to LA for the *Grammys* themselves, he wasn't flying in until tomorrow morning so he wouldn't miss more school than absolutely necessary. As a result, I was sure Carter would be completely indisposed tomorrow night. Even though Chase and Carter had only been apart for a few days since the holidays, tomorrow would be the last time they saw each other for a while.

We headed to the back entrance of a restaurant a few blocks away. Carter had chosen this place as it had a reputation for providing discreet service to public figures. It was crazy to think that the Thorns now fell into that category; at heart I was a military brat nobody. But our star had been rising steadily for a few years, and as the front man, Carter had to be increasingly careful these days.

"Thank you," I said to the host who seated us in a secluded, dark corner.

"So how was the cottage?" Carter asked after putting his menu down.

"It was good. Really good. Read some books. Walked along the water a lot. Played with a new song or two."

"Can I—"

"No, they're not ready for you to hear them," I said with a laugh, cutting off Carter's request. He had always been the most passionate about new music, and it didn't surprise me in the slightest that he was excited to hear that I had been writing. Even though the plan was to bring Chase onboard as our main songwriter, I still wanted to contribute when the right inspiration struck.

"Had to give it a shot," he said, exaggeratedly snapping his fingers in defeat. We grinned at each other, knowing there was no animosity meant by the exchange.

"How about you? We talked on Christmas, but I wanna hear about Paris with your guy. Anything I should know about?" I wiggled my ring finger suggestively.

Carter chuckled and blushed a little.

"Nah, not yet. Don't want to push things too soon. Maybe this summer, though," he said.

"Aww, really? That's so exciting, Cart. I'm so happy for you two."

It was crazy to think my best friend was contemplating getting engaged. It had only been a year ago that he came out onstage and told the world he was in love with Chase. A year exactly, now that I thought about it. I guess this weekend served as an anniversary of sorts. The thought made me smile.

Those two fit together like no other couple I had ever seen. They'd had a little bump in the road before we went out on tour in the fall, but they were able to work it out. I was sure it must be incredibly difficult for them not to see each other for months at a time, but Carter and Chase had the epitome of a trusting relationship and they were clearly both in it for the long haul. Plus they wrote awesome music together. A win-win if I'd ever heard one.

"Yeah, I've been thinking about it. Proposing sounds scary as fuck."

I laughed at the grimace on Carter's face. Like there was any way in hell Chase would say no when Carter found the balls to ask. Our conversation veered in other directions as our food came. I had ordered a vegetarian pasta, and it tasted incredible relative to all the crap I had been eating lately.

"So what was up this morning with the choreographer guy? You know each other?" Carter asked around a bite of chicken.

Shuffling the noodles around on my plate I contemplated how much to say. I sighed and decided to go for the truth. Maybe Carter would have some advice on how to handle this situation I had somehow gotten myself into.

"Yeah. It's kinda a long story," I said.

"I've got time," Carter replied with a kind smile.

"Remember that talk at Juilliard that Chase asked me to do back in October? With the first-year piano students?"

Carter nodded.

"Well, when I was done speaking, I got turned around trying to get out of the building and ended up in the dance wing. "Galaxies" was playing down the hall, and I got curious, so I wandered into the room I heard the music coming from."

When I had first written "Galaxies," I told Carter, Dean, and Ash about the meaning behind the song. We had never publicized the story, and to our knowledge nobody outside the band knew the tune's origin. Or at least they hadn't until Jamie's dance had become a thing.

"This guy was by himself. Dancing. It took my breath away it was so beautiful."

"Jamie?" Carter guessed, smiling over his water glass.

I nodded.

"He recognized me immediately and said he was having some troubles with the ending, asked if he could pick my brain over a drink. We got to chatting. I told him the song was about a guy—and the basics of all that bullshit—and I guess that was exciting for him to build the dance on."

Carter opened his mouth as if he was about to say something before shutting it again. I took a drink, hesitating on the last bit.

"And then one thing led to another," I finished with an awkward laugh.

Carter's eyebrows shot up like he hadn't expected that last bit. I shrugged my shoulders in a mock display of guilt.

"He's fucking hot. What was I supposed to do?"

"Wow." Carter exhaled. "That was a lot of information all at once."

I chuckled again, not knowing what else to say.

"And have you talked to him since?"

"No." I shook my head. "But then today on the lunch break…." I trailed off, trusting Cart could figure out the rest.

He threw back his head with a laugh.

"He's a great choreographer," I said. "He would have been fine on his own, but the dance would have been a straight couple and probably wouldn't have gotten the recognition it sounds like it's getting now if I hadn't said anything. I didn't even know he finished the piece until I saw him today. Had no idea he'd changed it to two guys or that it went viral."

"And you're okay with that? Don't feel like he outed you or anything?"

Carter's concern gave me pause. I knew he always had my back. Nevertheless, hearing him say things like that reminded me how much I could rely on him. Between my dad and my shitty exes, I'd never had many people in my life I could completely trust. Carter was one of the good ones for sure.

"No, I don't feel outed. Hardly anybody knows it was me who wrote the song or that it was written with a guy on my mind. For all they know, it's only Jamie's interpretation of the lyrics. But honestly I wouldn't care if people did know. I'm not in the closet with people that are actually in my life, I just don't want the world prying into my bedroom."

Carter nodded thoughtfully. "So you gonna one-thing-leads-to-another him again?" he asked with a teasing grin.

"As soon as we're done here, darling." I winked.

He laughed and made a theatrical motion for the check.

"Then let us get you the fuck out of here."

Jamie

I PACED the plush carpet floor of my hotel room, anxiously waiting to see if Beau decided to show up. Attempting to distract myself, I had already eaten, watched some uninspiring crap on TV, and had a shower. I had no idea how long the sound check would go on or if he would have other obligations after. He should have been here by now if he planned on coming, right?

What was with me? I was never this jittery and nervous with guys.

Even with all the time I'd had since the dance part of the rehearsal had been completed, I hadn't given a lot of thought to what I wanted when Beau actually arrived at my room. I mean, besides the obvious.

While I had thought about the sex we'd had back in October a lot since then—*a lot* since then—I had also thought about our conversation in the bar. And the sweet way Beau had buried his face into my chest in the alleyway, looking for comfort. And the pancakes he'd made me in the middle of the night. I liked talking to him. We got along so well that evening, and clearly our chemistry was off the charts. After the care he took with the dance floor today, it cemented the voice in my head that insisted these were not things that casual hookups did for each other. I hoped we had a chance to hang out and talk tonight as well as the other stuff.

I almost jumped out of my skin when I finally heard the knock on my door. My body flooded with adrenaline, and I thought my heart was going to pound its way out of my chest. I took one last glance in the full-length mirror and smoothed an invisible wrinkle out of my hoodie. When I looked through the peephole, I saw Beau running his fingers through his hair as he waited. That made me grin, realizing he was as nervous as I was. He was wearing the same gray T-shirt from earlier, but the light made his jeans look darker. I liked that about Beau. He was probably extremely well-off due to the success of the band, but nothing about him seemed pretentious. He played keys instead of asking for a fancy grand piano. He made breakfast instead of ordering us an elaborate meal. He wore a simple gray T-shirt instead of an expensive designer brand.

"I hear you breathing on the other side of the door, Jamie. Fucking let me in already."

He spoke his mind instead of blowing smoke up my ass.

Laughing as I unlocked the deadbolt, I drew the door open so Beau could step inside my room. My eyes fell to the sexy curve of his lower back and the perfect shape of his ass as he walked in front of me. Fuck. I wanted nothing more than to finally see his body in all its glory.

"How was the rest of the rehearsal?" I asked.

"It went well," he said. "We're playing two other songs. No other surprise guests arrived, so I decided to take you up on your offer of tonight."

"Oh yeah? You were holding out for Travis Wall or something?"

He shrugged his shoulders noncommittally. "Eh, nice to keep my options open."

I narrowed my eyes. I knew we were teasing each other, but I *did not* like the itchy feeling of jealousy crawling up my body. I took a step closer to where he was standing by my bed—a lion stalking his prey. His breaths became louder. The heat of his glare set me on fire.

"Fuck your options," I growled and captured his mouth in an aggressive display of ownership.

It was hard and impatient. All teeth nipping and tongues stroking against each other. He wanted me as badly as I wanted him, and I fucking loved that he wasn't afraid to show it. For someone who had as much raw power as Beau, it was such a turn-on to know he could flip and be completely submissive when he craved playing that role. Knowing that he didn't need to let me take control, he *wanted* me to.

I kissed my way down his neck. As much as it pained me, I held back and made sure not to mark him anywhere visible before the ceremony tomorrow.

"God, I love how you kiss," he said as I snaked my hands under his T-shirt and all but ripped it off him.

Once it was gone, I pulled back just enough to admire his naked torso. I ran my hands over the miles of his fair skin. His strong shoulders. His defined musicians' forearms. His flat stomach. His ruddy nipples.

Beau closed his eyes in pleasure and gave a sexy little gasp.

"Like that?" I asked, my voice having an unintentional growl in it.

"Uh-huh," he moaned.

I played with one nipple slowly, teasingly. Circling the dark skin I watched the reaction of pained pleasure on his face. I wrapped my other arm around Beau and held him against me. His breathing was shallow and labored. His cock was steel against my leg. I ghosted my lips back to his neck at the same time as I pinched his hard nipple.

"Oh God." He buried his face in my neck.

I continued tweaking and rolling the bud between my fingers, listening to his symphony of moans as the tormented skin grew hot and bright red. Beau's hips began to thrust against me, frantic for pressure on his needy cock. I pushed him toward the king-size bed, crawling up his body immediately after he fell. Finding his other nipple with my teeth, I bit down, and his back arched off the bed. I soothed the abused flesh with my tongue, licking and sucking and doing anything else I could think of. The sounds Beau made were desperate, and I decided to take mercy on him—at least a little.

With my lips on his chest, I trailed my fingers down blindly, searching for the buttons on his jeans.

"Well, well, well. What do we have here?" I teased him as I popped the top button and slid the zipper down easily.

"I knew you were going to be here this time," Beau said, referencing our escapades earlier in the afternoon.

I groaned as I pushed his jeans over his hips, realizing that not only had he changed his pants to make for easier access, but he also hadn't slowed things down by wearing underwear. Christ, it turned me on to see his shaft encased in only a thin layer of denim.

Once his jeans were gone, I took a moment to simply stare at the glory of my rock star laid out naked and hard for me on my bed. The power dynamic we both loved was evident with me fully dressed and him not wearing a single stitch of clothing. I ran my hands up Beau's calves, drinking him all in. Kneeling between his parted legs, I looped the tip of my tongue up his thigh and into the crease of his groin. His skin smelled musky and masculine; the coarse hair tickled my nose.

Pulling back slightly from the juncture between his legs and his hips, I yanked my hoodie and T-shirt over my head quickly and tossed them behind me on the floor. Beau immediately sought my skin. I relished his hands on me, enjoying and worshipping the body I worked so hard to maintain since I'd stopped dancing every day.

After planting openmouthed kisses up his torso, I brushed his bottom lip as I circled the dripping head of his cock with my thumb. Christ, he got so wet. Beau's hands pushed at the elastic fabric of my athletic pants, trying to find purchase to rid me of them. I took pity on him and slid the fabric over my hips. My blue briefs were all that remained between us.

I continued to stroke Beau's cock and kiss his pink lips, loving the feeling of his body growing tenser, his muscles jittery and strained.

"Fuck, I could come from this," Beau said against my mouth.

"Better not," I warned him. "I've got other plans for you."

Beau

JAMIE was absolutely going to kill me tonight. I had been embarrassingly close when it was just his fingers and his lips on my nipples. Fuck. How hadn't I realized how much of a turn-on that was before? And now with his hands on me and actually feeling his skin on mine for the first time? It was almost too much pleasure, and we'd barely even done anything yet.

"Fuck, I could come from this," I said.

"Better not. I've got other plans for you."

I shuddered at the implication as Jamie unexpectedly pulled his hand off my cock. I let out a groan of protest at the loss of contact. He chuckled at my objection as he removed his weight from me and stood up next to the bed. The move put his straining royal blue briefs directly in my line of sight. I licked my lips as he dipped his finger into the elastic to tease me. My entire attention was focused on the black band and the shape of his fingers as he slipped them inside the fabric.

"Mmm." Jamie breathed a sigh of relief as I watched the outline of his hand wrap around his hard cock. He stroked himself slowly and threw his head back in gratification. Subconsciously, my hand moved down my abs and went to grip my own member.

"No," Jamie said. His head snapped forward and his eyes glared forcefully at me when he noticed what I was doing.

I froze at the command and immediately let go of myself. A whine fell out of my throat.

"Oh, baby. Don't worry. I'll take care of you so good."

I nodded, feeling my body relax at his calming tone and unconditionally believing every word. He moved my fingers to his cock; he didn't let me touch him inside the fabric yet, but feeling his thick, curved length in any capacity was incredible. I stroked and played with it, enjoying the weight in my palm. Finally—*finally*—he tugged off his briefs and I got a look at his whole body naked for the first time. And what a fucking sight it was. I had seen his chest on the day at Juilliard when he was dancing, and obviously I'd seen his cock a couple of times now. Nevertheless there was something so intimate about him being fully on display like this.

Jamie kissed me softly. Thoroughly. Never letting me forget who was in charge. He lay down on top of me once again, rolling his hips into me and ramping up the urgency until I was moaning around his tongue. His fingers snuck between my legs, below my tight sac, and started to rub against my taint.

Oh God. Oh yes.

I spread my legs wider, encouraging him to keep going. The digit circled my ring before filling me in one stroke with a delicious burn. Jamie reached behind him to open a drawer in the nightstand, finding a new box of condoms and a tube of lube.

"Planned on this?" I asked.

"Hoped for it after this afternoon," he said with an easy smile as he warmed up a few drops of the lube. "You sure about this?"

I looked into his eyes with what I hoped was desire and said the one word I knew would get me anything I wanted with this man.

"Please."

Jamie let out a long-drawn-out moan and added a second finger, stretching me quickly. Considering the amount of time that had passed since I'd last had anal sex with a man, I should have asked him to slow down a little and prep me more. But that would have meant waiting.

He tore the foil on the condom wrapper with his mouth and unrolled it over his swollen cock, wiping the excess lube on the outside. I used the second while he was busy to flip over to my hands and knees, knowing I needed him as deep inside me as possible. Jamie ran his hand over the curve of my ass, taking stock of what I was offering him before propping my hips up and sticking my butt out even more. I felt the pressure of his hand on my shoulder blades as he pushed my face into a pillow. Fuck, it was such a slutty position he'd put me in. If it was anyone other than Jamie, I might have felt uncomfortable, but all I could do was whimper and beg him to use my body. My fingers scrambled for purchase on the bedsheets as he aligned his cock with my hole and... held it still.

Just fucking stopped.

I unconsciously held my breath. The light pressure he maintained was enough to tease but not enough to penetrate. I sensed its weight against me, heat radiating through the latex. It's like I could feel each individual nerve ending in my body waiting for him. I groaned desperately.

"Jamie, please!"

I was going crazy. I needed him to do *something*.

"Go ahead, rock star." He chuckled—fucking chuckled!—at my desperation. "I'm right here. Take what you need."

The permission was barely out of his mouth when my hips started moving back of their own accord. Jamie sunk into me, inch by inch. He held my hips steady, governing my movements even when he let me believe I was in charge. My back started to break out with sweat as he filled me. My breathing was unsteady and ragged. Jamie gave me a second to adjust when I felt his short pubes tickle my hole.

"Dammit, Beau. You're so tight."

I tensed my muscles, hoping to earn more of his praise. In my position I couldn't move much, but I could do that. After a beat, he pulled out nearly the whole way and pushed back in epically slowly.

The leisurely, breath-stealing strokes were the opposite of everything we had done together before. All of our other times had been urgent, frenzied. I wanted him no less than before, but the pace made the sensations incredible in a completely different way. Each spot he grazed seemed to be an erogenous zone of its own. I felt every inch of him as he completely owned my body. It wasn't like the sex was particularly emotionally driven or tender; if anything the glacial pace Jamie set was more of an additional measure of command.

He picked up speed, though it was still not nearly enough. I was convinced he was purposely trying to drive me to the brink of insanity. My body felt heavy, and my arms began to shake from holding me up. He pulled my cheeks apart with his hands. I looked over my shoulder to see him staring down at our coupling. Jamie watched himself thrust into me, disappearing into my body over and over. He groaned as his tempo became more irregular and he seemed to fight himself for control.

"Fuck. Beau. I'm gonna... fuck."

Jamie grabbed my hips hard enough to bruise. He drove himself into me one last time as he cried out. Still buried inside me, Jamie sought out my mouth for a demanding kiss. The angle was awkward, but the dual feelings of his tongue and his cock made it worth it. I was aching for my own release, but I trusted Jamie to take care of me. Jamie coaxed me onto my back, his softening dick falling out as I moved. He quickly tied off the condom and dropped it into the trashcan under the nightstand. Moving down my body until he was level with my neglected shaft, he kissed my hip bone. I wriggled and moaned in desperation for release.

"Need something, rock star?" He asked with a wink.

Before giving me a chance to respond, he licked around one of my balls and sucked it into his mouth. I gasped loudly, and he used that opportunity to fill me with two of his fingers. They massaged and stroked, searching for that special place that felt so g—

"Oh fuck!" I cried out.

Found it.

Jamie continued to rub me with his fingers, and then without warning he had his lips around my cock too. Fireworks shot behind my eyes, and I was spilling into his mouth before I realized what was happening.

When my heart rate returned to normal, Jamie kissed up my chest and onto my cheek. He ambled into the bathroom to clean up, bringing me a wet towel and taking care of me afterward. He slipped under the covers, and we relaxed against each other, spent from the day and from the workout.

After an hour of sleepy, happy conversation and cuddles, Jamie drifted off. I looked over at the gorgeous redhead snoozing beside me and couldn't help but want more. *More* was basically impossible. It didn't make any sense given I would be back in Europe in a matter of hours and he would go home to New York City. I had a horrible track record with men. I barely knew him.

But everything I did know about him made the wanting-more feeling grow. He was driven and talented. He was hilarious and sexy and unafraid to be himself. He was an artist, and a completely unpretentious one at that. He was kind and careful with my body, even when I begged him to push its limits. He took care of his dancers, gave them opportunities he never got himself.

Our situation hadn't changed from that first night. For him it was sex, nothing else. The lines were simple here, and I refused to let myself waste the rest of the tour pining over a hookup. I was starting to feel attached, and that had never ended well for me in the past.

No, wanting more with this incredible, beautiful man was an impossible fantasy. I would never be worthy of someone like Jamie.

Some people were meant to be alone.

Sighing resignedly, I tiptoed around the room, found my clothes and dressed silently. Jamie barely stirred at the click of the hotel room door as I slipped into the empty hallway.

Jamie

I WOKE up alone but okay. Irritated, but *okay*. It was the day of the *Grammy Awards* and I had too much to worry about without adding a certain brown-eyed rock star on top of everything else.

Beau and I'd had a great night last night. A *fantastic* night, if I was being honest. I couldn't figure out why he had left. I tried not to overthink it or take it personally. Maybe he wanted his own space or needed to make sure he slept before today, but the insecure part of my brain made me wonder if he still only saw me as a groupie or an easy lay. And that pissed me off. Beau and I hadn't made any promises to each other. Not even close! What right did I have to be upset that he didn't stay the night? I didn't even have his phone number for Christ's sakes!

So I pretended to ignore the bitterness and the feeling of being used, the hurt of being left alone. Beau was a distraction, and tonight was a huge deal for my career. My choreography was what had gotten us here.

No, a cynical voice inside my head chastised me. *Beau's song and story are the reason why you're here!*

If it hadn't been for meeting Beau, the dance would have remained a typical male/female pas de deux. It would have gone over fine at the Juilliard showcase and probably never would have seen the light of day after that. The only reason I was at the *Grammy Awards* was because I had stolen Beau's storyline of two guys. This huge event in my life was irrevocably intertwined with Beau Davis. I had complicated it by sleeping with him, and now I was upset that he intended to keep it simple and only sexual.

I tried to practice some yoga to calm myself down. Then I ordered a huge plate of eggs benny from the room-service menu and watched someone trying to choose a house in the Caribbean on the massive TV screen.

I may have overreacted and thrown a napkin across the room when they picked the wrong one.

Moving on.

I took a long, hot shower. Tidied up my beard. Put some product in my hair, threw on some shorts and a T-shirt, and stuffed my feet into my sneakers. Grabbing my phone and my sunglasses, I headed outside to wander around LA to clear my head.

A few hours later, after some sunshine and retail therapy, I felt slightly better. My phone rang as I was maneuvering all my shopping bags back through the door to my room.

"Hello?" I answered.

"Hey, Jamie, it's Claudia."

"Oh hey! How's it going back home?"

"Good. Everything's fine. I wanted to call to say 'merde' to you, Hayden, and Reece before tonight. It's a huge thing you're doing, and the whole department's super proud of you all."

I smiled to myself that Claudia would take the time to call. Saying "merde"—the French word for "shit"— was typically the way dancers wished each other well prior to performances. We were nothing if not a superstitious lot, and saying "good luck" to someone was horribly unlucky.

"The *whole* department?" I asked, raising my brow skeptically. "I can think of one person who is probably rooting for actual broken legs."

I sat down on the bed and pulled off my shoes.

"Yes, the whole department. Coleman's only bitter because you're thirty years younger than he is and he's never done anything this big."

"Well, I'm sure that's not the only reason he's bitter toward me. But I appreciate the call and the support. Hayd and Reece deserve all the accolades they get, and they're going to rip up the stage tonight. Watching them rehearse yesterday with the band live was insane. It's giving me so many ideas."

"That's awesome, Jamie. I'm sure this is just the start for you. You've got a powerful artistic vision, and clearly your work speaks to people. Anyway I don't want to keep you. We're throwing a viewing party tonight in the theater, so we'll all be watching and cheering you on. Plus that music composition student is nominated for the other Inevitable Thorns song. Gonna be a lot of pride for Juilliard. I'm looking forward to hearing all about it when you get back."

"Thanks so much, Claudia," I said sincerely. "See you in a couple days."

I hung up the phone feeling better. Claudia's comment about my viewpoint and connecting with the public tumbled around my head. Even if the song and concept were Beau's, Hayden, Reece, and I had added our voices to it. The dance was our stamp on the song like the uniqueness each musician in the Thorns brought with his own instrument. A dancer's work could not exist without a song first, and in a lot of ways we *relied* on musicians. Maybe that was why I was so enamored with the concept of a live band and dancers sharing the stage. Maybe that was even why I loved choreographing to raw, unconventional, and emotional music. The concept excited me. I would need to muddle that through later, see if more interartistic collaborations were something to consider.

But tonight… tonight I had other things to focus on.

I took a breath and began to get ready for the big event.

Beau

"AND the winner for Best Song is... Laila Summers for 'Wanna Wake U Up.'"

I let out a disheartened breath around the tight, fake smile plastered on my face. The cameras were still on my bandmates and me, and we clapped and cheered professionally for our competition. We had met Laila a few times at recent events, and by all accounts she was a massive diva. Her music was catchy, if you ignored the fact that it required more Auto-Tune than actual vocals to be palatable. There was a down-low bet going on tonight about whether Laila would get caught lip-syncing her live performance.

The red light of the camera in my face went out, and the operator moved on as Laila made a dramatic show of running to the stage in tears to accept her award. I reached beside me to touch Chase's hand, wanting to make sure he wasn't too disheartened. On the other side of Chase sat Carter. Their fingers had been intertwined all night, and their grip now looked white with tension.

"You okay?" I whispered to Chase, giving his hand a quick squeeze before letting go.

"Yeah. It was a long shot anyway. Besides, 'Next to Me' winning last year turned out to be far more important," Chase said, smiling.

His eyes were soft as he gazed down at his hand, linked with his boyfriend's. Carter shot Chase a look that was a cross between wonder and overwhelming love.

The two really were unbearable.

I checked Dean and Ash, who were sitting on the other side of Carter. Dean shrugged his shoulders, and Ash and I exchanged disappointed smiles. We were all saddened by the loss, but we would be okay.

There was no relaxing after the winner had been announced in our category as in the following commercial break, a PA approached and pulled the four of us backstage to prepare for our set.

I had worn a navy suit to the event, with a white button-down underneath, knowing it would be an easy outfit to perform in without going through the hassle of changing clothes completely. Backstage in the dressing room, I pulled off the jacket and undid an extra button at the collar of the shirt before turning the sleeves up to my elbows. I spent a minute or two fixing my hair; that would have to suffice as my performance look. As I finished, a voice over the sound system called Inevitable Thorns to the stage, saying we had five minutes before going on. We hadn't actually performed at last year's ceremony, and being asked to play not one but three songs was a really big deal.

I opened the dressing room door, glanced in the mirror to do one final check of my hair, and stepped into the cinderblock hallway.

"*Oof*," I heard at the same time I felt my body smack directly into someone in the hall.

I cursed myself for not paying attention and hoped it wasn't a big-name celebrity I had inadvertently collided with. Taking a step back, I realized it was even worse than barreling into Beyonce.

"Oh. Hey," Jamie said with an uncomfortable smile.

"I'm so sorry. Are you okay?" I asked. I ran my hand through my hair nervously before realizing I had messed up my locks again.

"Yeah, I'm fine." Jamie's voice was clipped, not the warm, teasing sound I was used to. I furrowed my brow, unsure about how to proceed.

We stood there awkwardly.

"I wasn't paying attention," I said. "I should have been… paying attention."

I was making things worse. Though I was pretty sure Jamie was upset with me—likely for leaving without saying goodbye—he didn't understand the circumstances. It was better this way for both of us—cutting things off before I could get even more attached to him.

"Inevitable Thorns, three minutes. Three minutes. Please report to the stage."

I looked up at the speaker as if it were responsible for me feeling like an ass.

"Well, good luck, I guess. Or break a leg? Isn't that what theater people say?" I frowned, growing more uncomfortable the longer he remained silent.

"Or is wishing broken legs to a dancer too terrible to even say?"

His eyes flickered up from the ground to meet mine with a sad smile. A moment passed where we just looked at each other. I took a breath.

"I'm sorry," I said softly. He nodded, somehow knowing I was apologizing for leaving instead of for my current babbling unease. "Can we talk later?"

"Beau Davis to the stage immediately, please. Beau Davis to the stage." The authoritative voice on the speaker sounded slightly panicky this time as she called for me specifically. Oops.

Jamie smiled at me for getting scolded as I gave him an apologetic grimace. I walked backward for a few steps, unable to look away from the beautiful man who I had hurt without meaning to. Turning my back to him and moving quickly to the entrance to the arena, I heard him call from behind me.

"Merde," he said.

I stopped and turned back to him, confused.

"Dancers usually say 'merde' for luck," he explained.

I smiled in understanding, feeling the ice crack by the tiniest fraction.

"Merde," I repeated, wishing him luck in his own language. He laughed quietly and pretended to tip an imaginary hat in thanks.

I hustled to take my place, grinning the whole way.

Jamie

INEVITABLE Thorns played through two of their current chart-toppers while Reece, Hayden, and I waited anxiously in the wings. There was once again Marley flooring on the stage, which gave me butterflies. Hopefully that reaction wouldn't be a long-term effect of this weekend; that would absolutely be a problem for my career.

Beau looked like the true rock star he was, hammering away on his keyboard. He had an ease to his posture up there, and he was nothing like the nervous man I had spoken to by the dressing rooms. It relaxed me a little that I hadn't unintentionally messed up his performance right before he went on.

I didn't want to be upset at Beau; I was sure that I would get over it, if I wasn't already. It just hurt waking up alone after I had felt such a strong connection with him last night. Hopefully we would get to talk at the after-party we were all attending, though I wasn't really sure what I wanted to say yet. I was heading back to New York tomorrow, and I was pretty sure the Thorns still had at least a couple of months left of their European tour. That didn't leave us with a lot of options to stay connected.

As the band's second song wound down, the applause from the audience crescendoed. The stage manager lined Reece and Hayden up in the wings, and I followed them, resting one hand on either of their shoulders in the shadows, a sign of what I hoped was reassurance.

"How's everyone doing tonight?" Carter spoke into the microphone, addressing the crowd. A cheer rang out from the spectators, although it was a fancy affair and the noise level probably wasn't what it would be at during a normal Thorns concert.

"We're so grateful you invited us to join you all here tonight. We've got one more song that a few of you have been listening to lately, and we've put together a special surprise!" Carter egged the audience on; the volume built as more people understood where this was going.

After a moment or two to build up the tension, Carter continued into his microphone.

"Choreographed by Jamie Griffin, danced by the incredible Hayden Zhang and Reece Varga, we are the Inevitable Thorns, and this is 'Galaxies!'"

The lights dimmed and then faded to black. The crowd was the loudest I had heard them all night. Hayden and Reece took their positions on stage in the dark like the true professionals they were.

I was left on my own, shaking in the wings.

As the lights came up over the first chords of the song, the feeling was like nothing I had ever experienced before. The crowd shrieking for our work quickly quieted and turned respectfully silent. It was almost eerie. The band's melody rose, blaring emotion and strength. Hayden and Reece threw their hearts—threw everything they had—into the song for what was likely the most important performance of either of their careers. I stood on the outside but somehow also at the center of it all. Goose bumps formed on my arms as the first verse blended effortlessly into the chorus.

Reece was like a man possessed on that stage. He flew around and yet still epitomized precision as he drew on his extensive training. Hayden lifted and caught, fought and internalized, caused hurt and hid pain. They were dynamic and I was so astoundingly proud of both of them.

And then there was Beau. Beautiful Beau, who inspired all of this through his heartache. A song that was so personal and still affected him to this day.

My eyes welled, and tears began to overflow down my cheeks. My vision blurred, and I fought to see as the song built in intensity. All of a sudden, a small light from the audience appeared. I couldn't really tell what was going on for a second because of the water in my eyes, but quickly more lights began to emerge. The entire audience was shining the flashlights from their cell phones at the stage. Galaxies.

It was one of those moments that you reflect on later when you contemplate the magic of live performance and know that no identical experience will ever exist again. A moment where my work was being performed at one of the biggest events of the year, played by my favorite band—including the guy who was currently consuming all my thoughts—and connecting the thousands of souls in the audience as well as those watching from home. I stood there motionless as the song dwindled, transfixed by the headiness of it all, with fresh tears streaking down my face.

Hayden exited the stage first, remaining in character until he crossed the curtain line. He saw my expression and immediately fell into my arms and broke down as well. We held each other and cried, not caring about the stagehands around us or the sweat or his near nakedness. Hayden and I watched together as Reece took his final position, the lights fading on him perfectly. The roar of the applause was barely audible over the thumping of my heartbeat.

Abruptly, all of the bright lights of the theater came on as the show went to a commercial break. It was like a switch flipped, and everyone was jolted out of the moment before they were ready. Reece walked over to the two of us in a daze. As soon as he saw the state Hayden and I were in, he clung to us and the three of us stood in a ridiculous circle bawling our eyes out, the impact of what we had done hitting us all over again. While performing at the *Grammys* was surely a highlight of any musician's career, performing at the *Grammys* as a *ballet dancer* was truly an inconceivable and unprecedented honor.

"Thank you, Jamie," Reece eventually said, hiccupping a little.

People around us started to fly into motion to set up for the next segment, so we headed for the backstage hallway to get out of the way. Before we left the wings, I saw Beau looking at me from across the stage, where the Thorns had exited and congregated. His head was tilted as he stared at me, clearly concerned.

"You okay?" he mouthed.

I nodded with a massive smile despite the tears.

Yes, I was more than okay.

Beau

I *LOATHED* these fucking parties. The drama. The schmoozing. The self-importance. The pretending you don't hate the guts of someone who won an award over you.

Normally Carter and I suffered together, but— surprise, surprise—he stayed for an hour and then made his excuses and bailed so he could dick out his boyfriend. The bastard.

Not that I could really blame them. Carter and Chase were looking out over a long time apart beginning tomorrow morning, so I tried to not resent him for dipping. Ash was talking shop with another drummer, and Dean was putting the moves on the drummer's date. Who I was pretty sure was his sister, but probably not the best idea either way. In short, I was unluckily alone when Laila Summers cornered me.

She had this annoying technique of making it seem like she was praising me, but always turned it into a backhanded compliment or a way to stroke her own ego. Tonight it was all "You're so lucky you didn't have to deal with all the press in the winners room! They wanted to talk to me for hours!" or "The dancers in your number were so great. They really distracted from how pitchy Carter's vocals were." Girl, please. Carter sounded fantastic, and everyone from a mile away could see that her microphone wasn't even turned on. At least she won me $50 on the lip-sync bet.

Eventually Laila saw another sucker she wanted to talk to and I was free of her.

I spotted his red hair at the bar before I saw his face. While he was trying to get the attention of a bartender, I sidled up next to him.

Jamie was wearing the same steel-blue suit with black lapels as when I ran into him in the hall before we went onstage. He had a black shirt on underneath and a matching black bow tie. The suit was tailored perfectly; it looked like it was made for him. It was anything but a standard, boring outfit choice, and it made Jamie stand out in the best possible way. He was certainly not a man who played it safe.

"Buy you a drink?" I asked.

Jamie rolled his eyes at me. "It's an open bar," he said with a flirtatious smile.

The bartender interrupted before I could respond with a witty comeback. Jamie asked for a white wine, and I ordered the same.

"Can we talk?" I asked, putting myself out there as the bartender poured us matching glasses. "Maybe somewhere alone?"

Jamie nodded and led us out onto one of the balconies. It was a cool night by California standards, so the balcony was basically abandoned. I gazed out at the sand of Venice Beach and the dark water beyond.

"You look good tonight," he told me. "That's a great color on you."

Jamie's dark blue eyes shone in the starlight, full of sincerity and candor, set off by the hue of the suit he wore.

"Thank you. God, Jamie so do you. I meant to say that to you earlier."

He smiled at the compliment over the rim of his glass. Almost like he didn't want me to see it.

"And the dance! It was something special when it was you alone in the studio, but up there tonight? You're an incredibly talented choreographer."

It felt like I was laying it on thick, yet I meant every word I said. We had barely spoken the whole time we'd seen each other this weekend. That was mostly my fault; it was easier to see our connection as only sex if it was, in fact, only sex.

"The movement may have been mine, but the idea—the beautiful story—that was all you," he said. "It never would have gotten this far if you hadn't put the concept into my head. I felt so guilty when the video started to go viral, like I'd outed you or maybe you wouldn't want this for your song."

I shook my head, moving closer to him and putting my hand on his arm without thinking.

"The song wouldn't have been nearly as popular today without your dance. I don't feel outed. I don't care if people know I'm bi. It's not a secret. I just don't want my love life broadcasted in the media. And it would be, for a while at least."

"It's a beautiful song, Beau. Tragic, but beautiful."

"I thought you didn't understand the ending?" I asked, reminding him of the reason we'd started talking in the first place.

"I understand it enough to know he hurt you."

I took a slow breath and met his gaze.

"I have this habit of not letting go," I said by way of explanation. "Of clinging to someone or something even though I know it's destroying me. Of getting too attached and making more out of a situation than I should. Trying to fix things. I *like you*, Jamie. But I know what this is. We're both leaving in the morning. It's easier not to let myself hope it could be more."

"Can we be friends at least?" Jamie asked me. His eyes were serious and sad.

"I'd like that," I said, forcing a half smile I didn't feel.

We exchanged numbers, and he promised to text me while Thorns finished the rest of our tour. I was grateful we had cleared the air about this morning and that we both wanted to stay in touch, but the rest of the night felt burdened, both of us recognizing we wouldn't end up in bed together again.

Eventually we finished our wine and drifted back inside to join the party. Heaviness fell on me with the knowledge I would have to say goodbye to him at the end of the night, an uncomfortable longing for the man who was still standing beside me. The decision not to push for more was the right one but felt wrong. Friendship was a consolation prize.

Jamie

TWO weeks passed quickly after we got home from Los Angeles. Hayden, Reece, and I received dozens of accolades from the faculty and other students, to the point of it being a little overwhelming. The view count on the video shot up by millions after the *Grammys*, and I received requests for interviews, job offers, and even sponsorship opportunities. Everyone kept asking what I was going to choreograph next, but my students were my first priority, and settling back into my routine at Juilliard was kind of nice.

Most importantly, however, returning to work was a distraction from Beau. He was on my mind all the time. Our conversation at the after-party cemented that what I felt for him was much more than physical attraction. I connected with him like nobody else I had ever met. I wanted to be the one to take away his pain. To worship his body and his mind like he deserved.

But I respected what he'd said too. It *would* be incredibly taxing to be apart, and I didn't want him to be unsure about where he stood with me. Beau deserved to feel like he was the center of someone's world, not like he was gripping on to a relationship by his fingernails. I had no doubt I could give him that if I had the chance, but I wanted *him* to believe it as well. We needed to build a foundation that was more than mind-blowing sex—maybe spending the next few months apart was an opportunity to do that.

So we texted. It started off small. A sentence here and there. He asked me about my day. I told him about this crazy snowstorm we had. He told me about an interesting biography he was reading.

It quickly grew to longer conversations. In-depth stories about ourselves, discussions about art and philosophy. It was hard for me to turn off the flirt completely. However, I tried to respect Beau's wishes and keep it platonic. We chatted as the Thorns made their way through Britain; they had a huge following there and were spending almost six weeks in the UK and Ireland.

My freshman modern dance class was finishing up one day when I glanced toward the door and saw the unpleasant sight of Coleman Hale in the entryway. His class directly followed mine in this room on Thursdays, and like usual he was early.

"Good work today, everyone. Just a reminder that tomorrow I'll post the sign-up list for my partnering masterclass. It's not mandatory, but there's only eight spots, so if you're interested sign up quickly. I'll see you all on Tuesday."

The students began to pull on sweats over their dance clothes and throw things in their bags. They chatted with each other as they exited the room. Coleman took a step closer, waiting until everyone else was gone before he approached me.

"Partnering masterclasses, Mr. Griffin? I don't believe that's the discipline you were hired to instruct." Coleman shook his head patronizingly.

"There've been some requests," I said.

My back was turned to him as I powered down the sound system and unplugged my phone. To be honest, "some requests" was a huge understatement. I had been inundated with students of all years asking me to coach them in partnering since the video became a sensation. Not simply partnering, but unconventional partnerships that expanded beyond one male and one female dancer. Beyond any pop culture recognition, this is what I was most proud of with our sudden fame: people thinking outside the box of the traditional structure of ballet. It was something I desperately wanted to capitalize on and light a fire under the students while there was interest.

"Did Claudia approve it, or are you making up all your own rules now?" Coleman asked with a sneer.

God, I hated this guy. What gave him the fucking right to come into my space and question the terms of my employment?

"It was her idea." I looked up from the gear I was tidying with a challenging stare.

Try me, Coleman. I dare you.

"*Hmmph.* Well, don't start expecting everyone to fall all over your feet, Mr. Griffin. Fifteen minutes of fame is short-lived. Then you'll go back to being a nobody."

"That's where you're wrong, Coleman." I spun to face him, crossing my arms and pulling myself up to my full height.

"That's not the point, don't you get it?" I went on. "Sure, nobody will care about me or that dance in a few months. But it sparked something in people. People from all over the world who don't give a shit about ballet connected with that number! It united them. Made them feel like a part of something. Like they were represented. And not just LGBTQ people, but young people. Damaged people! People from different countries and different backgrounds. People that have been in love and been hurt and maybe ended up okay, but *maybe they didn't*. Ballet isn't all swan queens and children's fantasies. It's grit and determination, strength and storytelling. It needs to change to be relatable or it will *die*."

"And you think that's what I want?" Coleman raised his voice, controlled but the anger and frustration was evident. "You think I want ballet to die? Ballet has been my life for nearly fifty years. The classics you're so hell-bent on destroying are the core of what we are. You have no respect for what's important."

There was panic in the undertone of Coleman's voice. A fear, perhaps, that he would become irrelevant if the art form changed too drastically. Coleman—despite our tumultuous personal relationship and his animosity toward me—had been a great choreographer at one point. I didn't want to discredit his work or what he stood for; however, he was so averse to other opinions, it was almost impossible to help him see my side of the argument.

"I'm not saying that." I took a breath and tried to calm down. "Classical work is incredibly important, but contemporary is where the futu—"

"It's a fad!" He cut me off angrily. "You're corrupting these young dancers and ruining their years of training with these… gymnastics you choreograph. It's harming their bodies."

"It's not. My dancers are safe and well taken care of."

"Hayden Zhang was a promising pupil, and now his technique is—"

"Coleman, I'm done with this conversation. Hayden's technique is flawless in whatever style he's dancing. How he chooses to spend his career is his decision, not mine, and certainly not yours. You *will not* hold your resentment of me against a student."

I threw the last of my items into my dance bag and moved around Coleman to exit the room, shaking my head at him as I passed. The man was utterly impossible.

Beau

I YAWNED as I stirred some sugar into my coffee in the conference room of our hotel in Liverpool. It was far too early in the morning for us to be awake after a show the previous night, but Cory called a band meeting that was apparently urgent.

"Any idea what this is about?" Ash asked me as he reached for the coffee pot.

"No clue." I shrugged.

I took a sip of the hot liquid and grimaced at the quality. It wouldn't prevent me from drinking it, but you'd think if Cory insisted upon holding this meeting first thing, he would have at least found us some decent coffee.

Ash and I joined the others at the small table in the center of the room. Carter raised his coffee cup to me in a mock toast, which I returned with a smile.

"Morning gents," Cory started.

He stared at Dean, who had his head down on the table, somehow having fallen back asleep. Carter—who was sitting next to Dean—poked him in the side. Dean jolted awake with a start, kicking one of the legs of the table and shaking the whole thing precariously. I quickly held on to my cup so the drink wouldn't splash everywhere.

"'M up." Dean eyed Carter, clearly annoyed. "The fuck we doin' so early?" he asked Cory.

"Not my first choice either," Cory, ever the diplomat, agreed. "Listen, something's come up from management. An idea. There's a ticking clock on it, and they wanted to get your thoughts ASAP."

"If I say yes, can I go back to bed?" Dean positioned his head back down on the table.

"Go on, Core," Carter said, ignoring Dean.

"Management wants to capitalize on the 'Galaxies' popularity. The video keeps shooting up in views since the *Grammys*, and our socials have been getting a lot of requests from fans to see the dancers live. The song was never intended to become a single, but it's kinda doing it on its own now."

I put my elbow on the table and leaned on it, trying to hide the smile that was blooming across my face. Jamie had put so much effort into choreographing that number, and I was happy that his moment in the sun seemed to be extending beyond the *Grammys*. He deserved every accolade he got.

"So what's the plan?" Carter asked. He was our de facto leader and unquestionably the best businessman out of the four bandmates.

"They want the dancers on tour," Cory said.

I choked on a sip of coffee, sputtering and coughing to try to clear my airway. Carter's eyes shot to meet mine. His expression was a mix between concern and amusement. Ash furrowed his brow, looking back and forth between the two of us, surely wondering what the unspoken dialog was.

The adrenaline was coursing through my veins. Holy crap. Jamie on tour with us? For the remaining four months of the European dates? I wanted to pull out my phone and text him immediately, convince him to do it and give us an excuse to spend more time together. To see what could develop. I had been fighting this growing attraction to him, and maybe I wouldn't have to anymore. My head was buzzing with excitement, and all I wanted was to scream "Yes, yes, yes!" in Cory's face.

"Fine," Dean said. He drew an exaggerated check mark in the air before folding his arms under his head as a pillow and returning to his slumber.

Dean's lack of enthusiasm took the wind out of my sails a little. Whatever. At least he had agreed.

Carter rolled his eyes at Dean before returning his gaze to me carefully. He continued to address Cory, asking questions for my benefit and making it clear that this was somehow my decision. I often wondered if what I had with Carter was similar to what being in an adult relationship would be like. He and I could talk about anything, and the support I got from him seemed like something a romantic partner would provide. Not that I wanted Carter as a boyfriend, but, like, someone similar to Carter.

"So how would that look? It would be the *two of them* touring with us and dancing that one number every night?" Carter said, emphasizing the number for my benefit.

Oh.

I saw where this was going now.

We didn't actually need Jamie for Hayden and Reece to dance with us. Jamie wouldn't have anything to do, and he would be an extra body to house and feed. My face fell with this realization. It was still an interesting thing for the band—a way to work with other artists and to increase the profile of the tour—but it didn't really change much for me if Jamie wasn't included.

"Correct," Cory confirmed, staring at us all strangely, like he couldn't quite figure out what was going on. "The LA office wants to throw out an offer today. Hopefully they would join us in time for the Manchester gigs this weekend."

"I think we should do it," I said.

It hurt my heart a little that Jamie wouldn't be directly involved. Nevertheless it was an interesting opportunity for the band, and Hayden and Reece both seemed like cool guys.

Carter nodded in agreement once I had voiced my opinion. "Ash?"

"Yup, good with me," Ash said.

"Cool," Cory said. "I'll let them know you're in, and we'll see how quickly we can make this happen."

Cory picked up his ever-present phone and notebook off the table and left the four of us in the conference room.

"So what was with all the side-eye?" Ash asked, glancing between Carter and me.

I took a sip of my coffee, trying to find the answer to Ash's question at the bottom of my cup. It was annoyingly unhelpful. I had no idea what was going on with Jamie and me.

"Beau's banging the choreographer," Carter said.

"Dude! What the hell!" I raised my hands in mock anger at Carter, with a laugh. I didn't care that he had spilled the beans to Ash—and possibly Dean, depending on his state of consciousness. We were a one-for-all band, and if Hayden and Reece were joining the tour, Ash and Dean should probably know the truth anyway.

"And it's bang*ed*," I mumbled out the correction. "Past tense."

I tilted the coffee cup to drain it.

"Wait, the redhead?" Ash asked. Carter nodded vigorously like an excited schoolchild, his grin stretching from ear to ear. "Is *that* what was going on when you walked up to him at the rehearsal?"

I blushed a little, embarrassed that other people had picked up on the energy between Jamie and me.

"Maybe a little bit?" I said.

"Do choreographers have dancers' bodies too, Beau?" Carter asked with a wink.

"Does your boyfriend know you're thinking about Jamie's body, Cart?" I fired back. "But yes, this one does," I added after a pause.

Ash snorted a laugh and high-fived me.

I was egging my bandmates on, but I shivered at the memory of Jamie laid out naked on top of me. His abs had been so sharp it was a wonder they didn't cut into my skin. His strong arms were perfect for holding me down. Taking control. His ass in those little shorts he wore that first day… fuck.

I stood up to leave before thinking about Jamie's body made walking too difficult. Ash followed suit and pointed to Dean's sleeping form in an unasked question if we should wake him up.

"Leave him," Carter said. "Maybe he'll get lucky and a groupie will find him here."

I snapped a photo of Dean with my phone, and the three of us laughed silently as we snuck out the door.

"Serious question, though," Ash said as we waited for the elevator to go back to our rooms. "Chase and Carter last year at the *Grammys*. You and this dude now. We gonna find me a girl next year?"

"Well, it's either you or…." I gestured back at Dean in the conference room.

Ash rolled his eyes. "Jesus. If he finds someone before me, I swear."

The three of us were in hysterics the whole elevator ride to our penthouse suites.

Jamie

MY phone rang as I was getting ready to leave my office to head to my last course of the day: a third-year modern class. I didn't recognize the number on the call display, but that had been happening a lot since the "Galaxies" video took off.

"Hello?" I answered.

"Hey, is this Jamie Griffin?"

"Yes, it is."

"Hey, Jamie, it's Cory Anderson. I'm the tour manager for Inevitable Thorns. I think we met briefly a few weeks ago at the *Grammys*?"

"Oh yeah. Hey man, how's it going?" I asked.

I was immediately interested in what Cory had to say. There was nothing for him to be concerned about regarding Beau; to my knowledge Cory didn't know we were friends—or whatever—and even if he did, why would he care? I checked the time. If I was a few minutes late to class, it wouldn't be the end of the world.

"Good, good. Listen, Jamie, I'm gonna cut right to the chase here. Management's going crazy for the publicity of the 'Galaxies' video and the hype from the *Grammys*. They want Hayden and Reece to join the band in Europe for the rest of the tour. I'd like to make them an offer—today if possible. Do you know if they have representation, or what's the best way to make this happen?"

My jaw dropped wide open. I was literally at a loss for words. This would be a four-month contract for the guys, a multicountry European tour doing one fucking number a night and getting paid to play with the big boys. It was a fucking *incredible* offer. I was so happy for them. However, it wasn't my decision to make.

Juilliard frowned on students taking that long off their studies for gigs. A couple of days here or there was understandable given the industry, but this would mean taking the rest of the semester off. Like most athletic activities, a ballet career relied on a limited window when a dancer's body was at its peak. Hayden was in his last term, and there was no way he would want to stick around for another year at Juilliard to make up the lost time.

"Wow. Cory, that's such a great opportunity for them. Thank you for being open to including dance in the show," I said honestly, trying to buy myself some time to process.

"Don't thank me. It was management's idea, and the band agreed to it. I'm just the messenger. I can give you a couple of hours to think about it, but I really need to know by tomorrow if possible. We want this to happen ASAP to keep the momentum going. I'll email you the draft contracts so you can see the terms and talk to the dancers or their agents."

I nodded as if he could see me.

"Sure. I'll try to do what I can. I'll give you a call as soon as I have an answer for you," I said.

"Cool. Thanks so much, Jamie. Appreciate it." Cory hung up before I could say goodbye.

I stared at my phone, stunned by what had happened. My feet eventually started moving and muscle memory led me down the hall to the dance studio. I saw Reece warming up along one of the walls, laughing with his friend Kiara.

"Reece, can I bug you for a sec?" I called over to him as I started to set up the sound system for my music. He jogged over to me.

"Can you get Hayden here for a minute when we're done with class? Text or call him. It's important."

Reece frowned at me, probably confused about why I would be asking.

"Sure?" he said, more question than answer.

"I'll explain after when both of you are here. Don't worry about it for now."

Ha! Don't worry about it. Simple.

I was distracted all through the class. My body was there—which I guess was the important thing—but my mind was elsewhere. I really shouldn't have been that fixated on my conversation with Cory. It would be huge to have my piece get that kind of exposure, but it wasn't like it was my decision to make. I thought about Beau and the part he might have played in all this. It didn't seem like it would have been his idea, though he and his bandmates certainly would have had to approve it.

I was desperate to text him and see what his side of the story was.

Class eventually ended, and true to Reece's word, Hayden was at the door waiting when I dismissed the students. I waited for the rest of them to leave and then sat down in the center of the room with Reece and Hayden, the three of us forming a triangle. The two dancers seemed nervous, curious why I would want to speak to them. At this moment all I was to them was their teacher. Conversely, the last time we had sat together like this was when I had gotten the offer for the *Grammys*.

"So," I started, "I got a call today from Cory, the manager for Inevitable Thorns. Apparently there's been a lot of requests to have you two perform 'Galaxies' with them. On tour."

"Holy shit," Reece said.

He and Hayden exchanged a look that spoke of both excitement and caution. I realized I had no idea if they were still together. If they weren't, they at least appeared to be on good terms.

"Yeah." I nodded. "Exactly. It's four months. Only one number per night, so it's a fucking sweet and easy gig. I looked at the contract briefly, and the money they're offering is ridiculous. But you'd have to work it out with Juilliard. Obviously I'll do what I can to advocate for you if this is something you wanna do, but I don't know what that would mean for you here. What we don't have, unfortunately, is time. They're looking for an answer tomorrow."

Hayden—always the logical one—nodded understandingly.

"It'd be an amazing gig. I want to say yes, but I can't lose my semester or risk graduation. I'm finalizing a contract for next year," he said.

"I thought that might be the case," I said. "We can talk with Claudia and see what our options are. Reece, what about you?"

"I'm… um, I'm not doing so hot in a couple of my classes," he admitted. "I'd like to make it work, but I think the admin's looking for an excuse to kick me out, and I don't wanna give them one."

Hayden picked up Reece's hand and kissed it reassuringly.

"We'll figure it out, babe," Hayden said, looking into Reece's eyes.

They leaned a little closer together, and Reece's shoulders relaxed. Well, I guess that was my answer about whether they were still a couple. I looked at the ground, not wanting to infringe on their moment. An uncomfortable jealousy roiled in the pit of my stomach as I watched them support each other. I should seriously not be jealous of my students' relationship.

I cleared my throat, bringing all three of us out of the moment.

"Okay, I'll set up a meeting with Claudia first thing tomorrow. I want you both to sleep on this. There's no pressure here if it's something you decide you don't want to do, regardless of what she says."

They agreed to think about the situation, and I cleared the meeting with Claudia's assistant before heading home. As I walked into my tiny shoebox apartment, I checked the time on my phone. Mentally doing the math and deciding it was late enough for the concert to be over, I pulled up Beau's number and called him. We hadn't spoken on the phone before, but

I didn't want to dick around with texting about this. By the third ring, I was preparing for the call to go to voicemail when Beau suddenly picked up.

"So I guess you heard the news?" Beau's voice had a smile in it.

"What, no 'hello?' No 'Good to hear from you, Jamie?' No 'How's New York?'"

"Why, 'ello there Jamie! So loverly ta 'ear from you, ol' chap. 'Ow's bloody New York this fortnight?" Beau asked, putting on an overly enthusiastic tone and the worst fake British accent I had ever heard.

I laughed at his dramatics. "That's terrible," I told him. "I guess it'll have to do, though."

"It's really good to hear your voice," he told me, dropping the pretense and verging on a dangerous amount of honesty. Not that I minded. It felt amazing to hear him say that.

"It's good to hear yours too." I felt my body relax with the confession. Like I had been holding tension I hadn't realized until the words came out of my mouth. I moved over to my double bed and lay down.

"So," Beau continued, pulling us back to the subject at hand.

"So," I said. "Hear you guys missed Hayd and Reece so much you couldn't go on without 'em."

"I wish it could be you," Beau said, and we were immediately back to the truthfulness that made me ache for a man I barely knew and wanted dreadfully.

"I wish it could be me too, rock star. But I wanted to thank you for approving this. It's a really big deal for the dancers."

"So they're coming, then?" he asked.

"They're not sure yet," I fiddled with a loose thread on my sweater. "We have a meeting with the admin at

Juilliard tomorrow morning. Both want to make sure it's not going to fuck with their academic standing first."

"That's smart. A degree from Juilliard is probably more important long-term."

I appreciated that he understood that. The tour was so exciting, but I didn't want either Hayden or Reece to lose sight of their education and future potential for the sake of one contract. No matter how high-profile and high-paying it was.

"It is. They're both driven young guys. Did you go to college?" I asked, changing the subject a little. It was so nice to talk to Beau, and I didn't want him to have an excuse to get off the phone as soon as we'd covered the highlights.

"Nah. We moved so much my grades were never very good in school. My family didn't have any money, so it wasn't something I thought about. I had a couple shitty jobs before Carter started getting us paying gigs and Thorns was making us some money. How about you? Did you go to college?"

"Yeah, I went to the Tisch school at NYU for dance, and then I did one year at teacher's college while I was rehabbing my ankle, knowing I needed to make a change long-term."

"Oh wow. I've heard Tisch's really impressive," Beau said.

"It's an investment as a dancer, for me as well as my students. To spend four of your prime dancing years in school is asking a lot. Worked out well for me, though, as I wouldn't have qualified to teach if I hadn't been to college. If you could have gone, would you have studied music?" I asked.

"No, I don't think so," Beau responded thoughtfully. "I think I probably would have studied something practical to get a reliable job. Maybe business or something with computers."

"And if you didn't have to be practical? When you were young, what did you want to be when you grew up?"

"I always wanted to study astronomy. I love looking at the stars, constellations, thinking about how big the universe is."

"Galaxies," I said, suddenly understanding. I smiled to myself. Astronomy. That fit Beau so perfectly.

He told me more about his love for space, and I listened with fascination. It was so refreshing to hear a performer speak passionately of something other than their art. Beau described how his mother used to take him stargazing when he was very young. How she'd bought him a telescope for Christmas when he was six, after saving up all year long. Through the phone I listened to his laughter and his reminiscences, wishing more than anything I could be there to hold him as he told his stories. To see the light in his beautiful eyes.

Beau's words grew slower, and his yawns punctuated the narrative more and more. I realized we had been on the phone for more than two hours. It must have been really late there.

"You should go to bed, baby," I said, the endearment coming out instinctively.

"Yeah." Beau yawned again. "Will you tell me how the meeting goes tomorrow?"

"I will. Good night, rock star."

Jamie

"NO! There is no way in fuck I'm letting him do this!" I stood up defiantly in Claudia's small office. The agitation brewing inside of me turned to full-blown anger, a side of myself I tried not to let my students or my boss see.

"Jamie, it's fine. I'm okay. Really." Reece tried to force a smile, despite the lifelessness of his eyes.

Hayden's hand scrubbed over his face in the chair next to Reece as I paced and continued to swear under my breath.

"I'm sorry, Jamie," Claudia said. "I have no option here. Coleman is Reece's program advisor and lead instructor. He has the authority to make decisions about outside contracts in this case. He *is* permitting Reece to take the contract, but Reece would not be permitted to return to Juilliard or continue his degree if he does so."

"But that's such bullshit! Doesn't he care about how amazing this would be for his student? It's a once in a lifetime opportunity, Claudia! You're the head of the department, why can't you outrank him?" I dragged my fingers through my hair, incredibly frustrated.

"Reece, Hayden, can you wait in the hall for a moment, please?" Claudia spoke to the two dancers with composure.

They obediently got up to leave, tossing me sympathetic looks as they walked by. Hayden closed the door to Claudia's office behind them.

"I wish there was something I could do," Claudia said. "You know how much I do. But it's political, and it's not my call." Her tone remained steady and authoritative, but the twitch in her eye let me know how difficult it was for her.

"It's a personal vendetta. He hates me. It's not fucking about Reece at all."

"Reece is on the border of failing out, Jamie," she continued. "The situation with Hayden is different. Hayden's a few months from graduating. He's at the top of his class and is being hunted by every artistic director in the US. You're his advisor, and as long as you approve this as his final production credit, he's free to go and will still finish school. Reece has another year and a half. He's a strong dancer, but the academics are a struggle. He's fighting for his life right now. I hate to say it, but I see where Coleman is coming from educationally."

I released a defeated sigh and let my body sag into one of the chairs. The adrenaline drained slowly from my system. I was fucking exhausted, and it wasn't even 10:00 a.m.

"So what are my options? Is there another student I can make the offer to?" I asked.

"Maybe? But do you really want that? Will the band want that? You cast those two so perfectly. Obviously they're smitten with each other. But that's beside the point. You said you needed to give the band an answer today. Can you teach someone that part in a few days on top of all their other classes?"

I groaned loudly. My molars felt like they were being embedded into my jaw with how hard I was grinding at them.

"There is one other option I see here," Claudia said, clicking her ballpoint pen a few times obnoxiously.

"Hmm?"

"You do it yourself," she said. "You know the part. The excitement will still exist from the band's perspective because you choreographed the piece to begin with."

My breath caught mid-exhale. Beau's voice played through my mind on repeat.

I wish it could be you.

I wish it could be you.

The hairs on my arms stood up, alive with possibility. There was no way it was this easy. I attempted to battle the excitement, not wanting to get too worked up before I had all the information.

"My job?" I asked, my voice small and far away in my ears.

"I might have an in with your boss." Claudia winked at me. "I can approve a professional development leave for you. We need you here long-term, Jamie. This is one semester. It's too good an opportunity to promote your choreography for you to turn down. This kind of publicity is positive for the school as well."

"I don't even know if I can do it physically," I said, depleting the last of the weak excuses I had. "My ankle is too wrecked to dance professionally."

"It's one number a night. You do more than that with the students every day and you know it. Keep up your PT and you'll be fine."

I nodded, knowing she was right.

"Holy shit." I laughed.

"You better go tell Hayden. They're so nervous out there the two of them look like they're going to pull something," Claudia said, gesturing out her big window to where Reece and Hayden were seated, holding hands.

While I was not looking forward to spreading the news to Reece that I was taking his spot, I hoped he would still see the big-picture opportunity here. It was obviously not ideal for Reece as a dancer, or for him and Hayden as a couple, but Reece was a smart cookie. He knew that dropping out of Juilliard wasn't going to do him any favors when he was looking to get picked up by a ballet company.

"Okay. Let me know what paperwork I need to fill out. I'll have to reschedule that partnering workshop for when I'm back. I promise I'll make it up to the kids next year."

As soon as I'd had the difficult conversation with Hayden and Reece—there had been tears, but ultimately they agreed that Claudia's plan was for the best—there was one call I needed to make before I let Cory know Hayden and I would be joining the tour.

When I dialed the number, he picked up almost immediately.

I smiled as I heard him answer the phone. "Hey, rock star. Guess what?"

Beau

I COULD barely wipe the smile off my face long enough to get through soundcheck. Jamie and Hayden had arrived late last night, and today was the first show they were performing in. The vast majority of the rehearsal had been for them: to get their lighting right, to make sure they had enough room to dance, and to verify the IMAG—the video cameras that projected onto large screens for patrons in the cheap seats—knew how to follow them properly.

Carter and Ash had been tossing me gleeful looks all afternoon. I wanted to throw something at them and tell them to be cool, although I had never been a very good actor and there was no way I was hiding my elation from anyone paying attention. Dean knew something was up with the three of us, but he'd been asleep the day Carter filled Ash in on my exploits with Jamie. So Dean remained entertainingly unaware and couldn't join in the teasing.

When Jamie told me Reece hadn't been permitted to take a leave from school for the tour, I had a pang of regret that we wouldn't be able to showcase his art on our stage. In the next breath, Jamie had explained how he would be covering Reece's part himself. I remember feeling… I don't even know. No phrase I could think of seemed sufficient enough to explain the elation pulsing through my body. Optimistic? Overjoyed? Was either word strong enough?

Jamie had been completely focused on dancing all day, which was probably for the best. When we spoke on the phone a few days ago, he was a little nervous about being able to perform to the same level Reece could. I thought he was full of crap. I told him that. Repeatedly. I had seen him that day in the studio at Juilliard. The feeling of my breath being stolen by how beautifully he moved was cemented in my memory. He may not be able to perform a full ballet anymore, but I had a feeling that if I had the pleasure of seeing him at 100 percent, I wouldn't be able to function. Jamie was a vision, and watching him now on the stage, a thin layer of sweat glistening on his skin and a determined look in his eyes, made it impossible to think he would be anything less than extraordinary.

There was this one time when I was young. We had moved to a new base, and I was upset about having to leave my friends—again. My mom took me down to the beach on a warm night in the summer, just the two of us. She brought us blankets and snacks I wasn't usually allowed to eat, and I remember lying against her. It was overcast all day but as it started to get dark, the sky cleared. We watched the stars come out. She pointed out the Big Dipper, the North Star, the Milky Way. I was fascinated by it all. And then, as I started to get sleepy and close my eyes, we saw them. Meteors shooting across the sky. It was magic. It was science. It was so familiar and also like nothing I had ever seen before.

That's how it felt when I watched Jamie dancing.

Beauty and wonder and light all mixed into one.

We finally finished the soundcheck and broke for dinner. The venue had brought in Indian food for us all, and we ate out of communal dishes in the greenroom. After I filled a plate, I went to find a chair at one of the tables. I couldn't see Jamie, but Hayden was sitting by himself, so I decided to get to know him a little.

"Mind if I join you?" I asked, sitting down without waiting for an answer and digging into my food.

"Of course not," Hayden replied. "Thanks again for including us. This is so insane to be here. I've never been anywhere."

"Thank *you guys* for getting us all sorts of free publicity on that song," I said with a smile. "How's it going so far dancing with Jamie?"

"He's heavier." Hayden and I both laughed at his joke. "Not in a bad way. He's just, like, taller and has more muscle mass than Reece."

"Yeah, I'm sure every pound makes a difference when you're doing crazy lifts like that." I paused to take a mouthful of the chickpea curry on my plate. "Sucks that Reece wasn't able to get out of school, though."

"Mmm. He's pretty bummed. But he's glad that we were able to make it work. Reece would've been sick if his shitty grades meant that the piece didn't get to come on tour at all. He idolizes Jamie."

At the moment Hayden said his name, Jamie appeared from down the hall. His hair was wet, so he must have had a shower in his dressing room before joining us for dinner. I was selfishly disappointed that all the sweat had been scrubbed off his skin. I tracked his body as he moved around the others and grabbed a light meal of rice and veggies before coming to sit with Hayden and me.

"Ready for tonight?" Jamie asked Hayden, rapping his knuckles on the table.

"Absolutely." Hayden grinned widely.

We ate and chatted amicably for a while. Hayden seemed like a good guy, and I wanted to make sure they both felt welcome, regardless if Jamie and I would stay just friends or see if there was anything more. God, I hoped there was more.

Dean came over and put a hand on one each of Hayden's and Jamie's shoulders.

"Dance friends, I have a proposition," he said.

"No. Say no, Hayden," Carter yelled from another table across the room.

I nearly shot the soda I was drinking out my nose.

Dean carried on, undeterred. "So you know that scene in *Dirty Dancing*? Where he lifts Sweetie over his head?"

"Baby," I corrected, rolling my eyes.

"Baby, Sweetie, whatever," Dean said to me. "You know when that happens?"

There was a long pause as Hayden and Jamie exchanged a look that was equal parts amusement and fear, knowing exactly where this was going.

"Yes?" Hayden said eventually, when Dean's raised eyebrows demanded an answer.

"I say we really mix things up at the end of the show. I'll come running down the front of the stage—"

"No. No, no, no, no, no," I said emphatically, cutting Dean off before he could finish his horrifying idea.

"Don't listen to the fun-downer. I'll start running, and then—"

"No. Final answer," Cory chimed in from the corner where he was sitting, typing away on his laptop. I hadn't even noticed him until now, but clearly our beloved tour manager had been paying attention—always a smart thing to do when Dean got a crazy idea in his head.

"Aww, come on! Core, when am I ever gonna get to do this again!"

"Hopefully never," Cory said. "We're already lucky to have Jamie filling in for Reece—thank you for that, by the way—we're not going to kill them both the first night with you jumping on them."

"Besides, if you injure them you gotta take their place in 'Galaxies.' Only fair," I said.

"I'd be a totally kickass ballerina. Ballerino? What are the dudes called?"

"How's this, Dean," Jamie chimed in. "I'll teach you some basic ballet. If I'm convinced you're not going to hurt anyone and if Cory's okay with it, on the last night of the tour we can *maybe* do 'The Time of My Life' lift."

"Deal." Dean shook Jamie's hand emphatically.

Carter and Ash cheered as Hayden snorted in amusement. Cory shook his head from the corner, but his lower lip fought a grin. He didn't say no. If nothing else, Cory was smart enough to know it would be a PR goldmine.

"First lesson tomorrow before soundcheck," Jamie said.

All the rest of us could do was laugh.

Jamie

I WALKED into my dressing room after dinner to get dressed for the show. I didn't have a routine down yet and wanted to make sure I gave myself more than enough time to primp and prepare. It had been so long since I'd gotten ready to go on stage and perform, I was terrified of forgetting something important.

I took a breath and then drank a long sip of the tea I'd made myself. My dressing room was one of the smaller ones. It was still private, which I appreciated. Sharing with Hayden was okay in a pinch, and I certainly didn't want to be a diva about the situation, but I was ultimately still his teacher, and I wanted to keep the lines as clear as possible between us. More importantly I had a feeling that my nerves would get the best of me tonight, and I didn't want Hayden to see me like that. I wasn't really a dancer, at least not anymore. My body had weaknesses now that it didn't have when I danced professionally. Dancers knew their bodies and their limitations extremely well, and I was under no illusions that I was in the best shape possible.

In the few days since I'd found out I would be taking this contract, I had worked my ass off to get primed. Back to the barre and the type of strength conditioning I had done early in my career. Well, not exactly. I wasn't pushing myself terribly hard. However it was still more formal training than I had done in years. My body ached all the time. I knew it would get better after a week or two as my muscles adjusted. Simply walking around these days after a good workout made me feel old.

My bet with Dean would probably help remind me to get to the barre every day. That was one of the main reasons I had agreed to the spectacle. Assuming, of course, he actually showed up tomorrow and followed through. I chuckled to myself thinking about the interaction and the prospect of doing the *Dirty Dancing* lift with him onstage. The crowd would fucking love it.

I took a seat at the vanity. It was a typical setup, with incandescent bulbs surrounding the mirror—making for much better lighting than the overhead fluorescents. I stared at my reflection for a long moment, as if to ask myself what the fuck I was doing. Running my hands over my short beard, I once again debated shaving it off. Reece had gone with a little stubble for his look in the part I was playing, but I wanted it to be clear that I wasn't trying to be a replica of him. Imitating what he had done would make me no better than the copy-and-paste jobs Coleman made a career of. The beard would stay, I decided.

Sorting through my Dopp kit, I pulled out a couple of products I planned on using. I pumped a tiny bit of hair gel through my locks, arranging them artfully. Debating makeup, I decided to only use a hint of highlight and shadow to emphasize the bone structure of my face. I pulled off my shirt and did the same to my abs. It was probably a little bit of false advertising. Nevertheless I was the moron who decided to make Reece and Hayden practically naked on the stage. I could use any help I could get. And also, Beau was here.

I felt a little nauseous as I heard the ominous countdown over the speaker in my dressing room. Ninety minutes to the start of the show. One hour. Half an hour with the house open. Thank God the Thorns had elected not to have an opening band on this tour. I don't think my heart would have been able to take waiting through another band before we hit the stage.

A knock sounded on my dressing room shortly after the half-hour call.

"Delivery for Jamie Griffin," a woman said once I pulled open the door.

She handed me a massive bouquet of flowers in a glass vase with a purple bow around it. I thanked her, and she left without saying anything further. The flowers were beautiful: roses and lilies, daisies and dahlias, and dozens of other blooms I didn't know the names of. They were magenta and blush, lilac and ivory, with gorgeous leafy greenery around the edges. I was completely touched by the gesture, and it calmed me a little to know there was someone rooting for me, though I didn't know who would have gone to the trouble to send me the blossoms.

A small card from the flower shop was stuck onto the front of the arrangement. When I opened the card, I smiled, immediately knowing who they were from based on the message inside. A single word.

Merde.

Beau

ANXIETY bloomed in my stomach as I paced in front of Room 913 at the hotel we were staying at in Manchester. I had been wearing a hole in the carpet for at least the last ten minutes, debating whether or not to knock on the door. Running my hand through my hair, I tried to psych myself up. It wasn't a big deal, I told myself. Totally not a big deal. Just fucking knock.

I had tried to track Jamie down after the show simply to check in. Carter hadn't seen him when I'd asked, and then he proceeded to tease me, which I should have seen coming. Eventually I found Cory, who said Jamie had caught a cab back to the hotel instead of waiting for the bus with the rest of us. I hoped he was okay and that he hadn't been avoiding me. Were the flowers I sent too much?

I sighed and rapped on the door lightly. It took much longer than I anticipated—enough time to skyrocket my apprehension—but eventually there were footsteps on the other side. Jamie opened the door, the back of his hand barely concealing his mouth, which was wide open in a yawn. He was dressed in red-and-black flannel pajama pants and a threadbare gray T-shirt. His red hair was sticking up at crazy angles. His right cheek was flushed and had a pillow crease. I felt like such a jackass. Of course he had been asleep.

Jamie opened the door wider so I could come inside. I immediately noticed the vase of pink and purple flowers next to the king-size bed, which made me smile. Maybe it hadn't been too much after all.

"Hey," he said once the door clicked shut behind us. His voice was gritty and deep; the sound made my dick twitch.

"Hey. I'm so sorry. I didn't realize you were sleeping."

He chuckled, scrubbing his hand over his face.

"Jet lag coupled with being out of shape," he said with a self-deprecating laugh. "Some rock star I am, huh? No parties, no groupies, couldn't even keep my eyes open long enough to take the bus home."

I smiled at him. He was too adorable for his own good when he looked so sleepy and soft.

"I wanted to check on you after the show, make sure you were happy with everything?" I ignored his comment about being out of shape because it was ridiculous. Had he even seen himself?

"It was… a dream come true, Beau. I don't even know how to describe it," Jamie said, waking up a little. He sat down on the bed and patted the spot next to him. I joined him—obviously, who could turn down that offer?—and he rested his hand on my knee. It took a second for me to be able to pay attention to his words again. All my attention was focused on the warmth of his hand.

"I never thought I'd dance again," Jamie went on. "And then to be able to dance in front of a crowd of that size? It was the biggest rush of my life. It—*this*—is all thanks to you. You're the reason why this is happening to me."

He looked deep into my eyes with sincerity and honesty. Without thinking about it, my fingers came up to his face to run over his prickly beard. He inhaled, almost on a gasp, at my touch. Jamie tilted his head as if he wanted to feel more of my hand on his face. His eyes fell closed, and he made a sound of pleasure in his throat. I stroked his cheek with my thumb, lost in the moment and unreservedly enraptured by his loveliness.

My heart pounded as I moved closer. I hesitated for a second, a hairsbreadth away from his mouth. It was a heady moment, and somehow it was more intimate than anything we had done before. He smelled like sleep and toothpaste and a little like a sweet fruit. Maybe a banana or a papaya—probably from his shampoo. My lips brushed his, a pillow-soft kiss that was everything I was craving in the moment.

As much as I longed to take things further, that one perfect kiss seemed to transcend the need for anything else. The little bubble we had built in the dark hotel room was intimate and cozy and seemed like more than I could ever deserve. How was I possibly lucky enough to get to kiss this beautiful man? Jamie sighed, and his eyes opened slowly, as if he didn't want to risk breaking the moment either. He smiled at me; it was sleepy and genuine.

After running my thumb over his jawline one last time, I pulled back the quilt on his bed so he could get under the covers. I stripped off my jeans efficiently, and crawled in with him in my boxers and T-shirt. His body fit perfectly against mine; my arm around his middle, my hips flush against his butt, our knees bent at the same angle. Despite the power games we both seemed to enjoy in intimate moments, getting to hold him as the big spoon seemed to feel natural for both of us.

A minute or two passed as I enjoyed the warmth of his body against mine. Just as his breathing had begun to even out in sleep, I heard him mumble, "Don't leave without saying goodbye this time."

My heart shattered at the honesty. There was no way I wasn't falling for this man.

Jamie

I WOKE up sweating profusely, an inferno of heat clinging to my side. And poking me with his morning wood. I smiled at Beau's sleeping figure and ran my fingers through his sandy hair. He mumbled something incoherent. Learning these little facts about my rock star satisfied me more than it probably should have. He ran hot in his sleep. That shouldn't have surprised me, because of how hot he was in general, but I liked that I knew that about him. I stroked his hip lightly with my thumb.

My gaze floated past Beau to the flowers on the nightstand. I thought about the kiss Beau and I had shared last night, which sucked all of the oxygen out of the room and lit my soul on fire. I thought about him being on his knees for me the first night we met.

I thought about the way he had influenced the dance I had choreographed.

I wanted more with him. I was past the point of denying it or making excuses to try to protect my heart.

Beau stirred a little, and his eyes fluttered and then slowly opened.

"Good morning," I said, batting my nose against his a few times gently before kissing the tip.

He slung his leg over my hip and pulled me close, making me groan when I felt his hard-on through the thin fabric of his boxers.

"Did you sleep well?"

He nodded and burrowed his head into my chest. Beau was a snuggler. I could absolutely get behind that. Wrapping my arms around him, I began lazily drawing patterns onto his back. He made happy noises as he started to wake up a little against me.

"Tell me about yourself, Jamie?" He asked me out of nowhere. His fingers scraped against my forearms soothingly. "I barely know anything about you."

"What do you want to know?"

"Anything you want me to know," he answered simply.

I smiled against his sleep-warm skin and thought about what to tell him.

"I started dancing when I was about eight," I said. "I remember I was always spinning around the living room when I was really young. It used to drive my parents crazy because I was never very coordinated, but they couldn't get me to stop. This one time, I had been watching a dance video and decided to try doing a *développé*—that's basically where you stand on one leg and extend the other to the side over your head. Anyway, I lost my balance and ended up kicking a side table.

The lamp on the table fell to the floor and shattered. Not my finest hour." I chuckled at the memory. "My parents and my older sister were all academics and they had no idea what to do with a kid who would rather do pirouettes than practice reading or math with them. When my mom and dad had me tested for ADHD and I met the threshold, things suddenly started making more sense to them. It fortunately hasn't affected my life as badly as it does for some people, although sitting still in school was always difficult. I had no interest in soccer or football, but I loved to twirl, so they enrolled me in ballet."

"Wow, that's so cool of them. They never questioned whether it was masculine enough?"

"Not once," I said, smiling. "My mom was a theoretical physicist, which is such a male-dominated field. I think she saw me dancing as a way to emphasize to me that gender barriers are bullshit. I don't know if they pieced together that I was likely gay or just thought of me as a boy who loved to dance. I didn't realize until a few years later that male dancers are some of the toughest athletes out there."

I took a second to enjoy the memory before getting to the tough part.

"When I was thirteen, my mom was diagnosed with ALS. She had noticed some weakness in her arms and cramping that was unusual. It seemed like nothing at first."

Beau took a deep breath, likely understanding how this story was going to end.

"She quit her job to spend more time with me and my sister, knowing how bad the prognosis of the disease was. She used to come to *every* performance I was in. Every rehearsal. At first she was able to walk, but then she started using a cane and eventually a wheelchair. But she never missed a single class. She used to say that I moved so much that I moved for her as well. That when I danced, I was her wings. She passed the day after my sixteenth birthday."

"Oh, Jamie," Beau said. He moved back to look into my eyes, and I saw nothing but support and concern in his.

"Dance makes me feel connected to her. When I got injured, I wondered if that meant I would lose her—the feeling of her—all over again. But honestly, that never happened. Whether I'm the one onstage or watching a piece I compiled, I know she's there."

"That's beautiful, Jamie. She sounds like she was a wonderful woman."

"She was," I said. "I've, um, I've never told anyone that before. It seems kind of silly, probably."

I tried to deflect the intensity of what I had said, not knowing if that was the kind of honesty he was expecting when he asked me to tell him about myself.

"I'm honored," Beau said simply, brushing a lock of hair from my eyes. "And it's not silly at all. I lost my mom when I was young too, younger than you were. It's probably easier that I barely remember her, but I understand what it's like to want to feel a connection."

"I'm sorry," I said. "I don't think there's ever a good time to go through that."

We lay together in silence for a while, each reflecting in our own heads. It was a comfortable peace, and I was grateful we could enjoy each other's presence without feeling the need to fill the quiet. A sense of mutual understanding washed over me. It was nice to know that Beau didn't judge me or think I was crazy for believing that my mom was with me when I danced. I was surprised that I had blurted that out; it wasn't my intention to even mention my mom when I began talking, yet somehow it felt natural. He stroked my hair, and I rubbed his back, and the world went on around us outside our safe haven. We would eventually have to get up and head to the theater for the second night of performances in Manchester. For now all that mattered was being with him.

"What is this, Jamie? Us?" Beau eventually asked.

"I don't know," I answered truthfully. "What do you want it to be?"

"I haven't had a great track record with relationships. I tried to not get attached but this doesn't feel casual to me. It hasn't for a while, to be honest."

"I feel the same way, rock star. So let's be more than that," I said simply. "At least while we're on tour."

"Are you sure that's what you want?" Beau asked quietly. He looked at me through his lashes, his eyes big and serious.

"I know I want you. That I haven't wanted anyone else since that first night in New York. I don't know what will happen, but there's this thing between us— this feeling—that I haven't felt before. I want to explore it. But this is your band, your tour, and I need to make sure you want this too."

"I do," he said immediately. So quickly that we both giggled a little at his enthusiasm.

"Do we... do we tell people?" He asked.

"I'm not really into hiding or sneaking around." I shrugged with one arm. "But again, this is a professional situation, and you know these people better than I do. As for the fans, that's entirely your call. I know you're not exactly out publicly."

"I'm not necessarily not out. More that I don't want the paparazzi butting into my life. I like the idea of not having to hide from anyone. I mean, you're okay to look at, so it's not bad for my reputation." He winked at me.

I ignored the ludicrous joke and kept the conversation on topic.

"Then we'll play it by ear. See what happens. When people know, they'll know. If we're doing this, the only thing that's important to me is that it's exclusive."

"That's more than fine by me," Beau said with an adorable half smile.

I kissed him. I couldn't resist. He was beautiful and sweet and sexy. Most importantly, he was mine.

Beau

I LITERALLY couldn't stop smiling. My teeth hurt, the muscles in my face hurt, but I could.... Not. Stop. Smiling.

It had been three days since Jamie and I had made things official. He had spent every day growing more confident in his dancing and in his place on our tour. And he'd spent every night in my bed. The sex was erotic and passionate and everything I needed. He made my body do things I had no idea it was capable of.

Everything was pretty much perfect. Nobody on the tour was surprised to see Jamie and me walking around hand in hand or getting caught staring at each other like we were the only ones in the room. We took a little flak from Hayden and Carter—both of whom were currently in long-distance relationships—for unintentionally flaunting being together. Ultimately we knew they were both happy for us, though Jamie and I agreed to try not to rub it in their faces.

We performed in Manchester and Leeds and then headed up to Newcastle for the next show. My phone rang as we were getting out of sound check. I saw my father's name on the screen and debated not answering. Sighing, I swiped to receive the call.

"Hello?" I answered.

"Hey, you forgot to transfer the money this month," my dad said. I was surprised that his voice sounded unaffected by alcohol. Maybe things weren't as bad as I had thought.

"I didn't forget, I just didn't send you any. I don't know why you need it if you and Joe both have jobs."

Since the incident at Christmas, I had unilaterally refused to send them anything. I had gotten a first-hand look at exactly where that money went, and I had no desire to fund their self-destruction with my hard-earned cash.

"We have expenses. You prob'ly make more in a day than I do in a month. Transfer it now, and make sure it's on time next month."

I reached for the back of my neck to rub the tension that had suddenly appeared. I heard some background noise on the other end of the line: a phone ringing, some women's voices. Ah, he was at work. That explained why he was more coherent than usual.

"Look, Beau," he said, "we need the cash. You're so damn selfish. Always have been. You mooched off me for a long time. You owe me."

"I don't owe you anything, Dad. Kids don't owe their parents for paying to raise them. And besides, I've given you more in the past year than you ever spent on us growing up."

"Don't talk to me like that you arrogant son of a bitch. Transfer the money right damn now."

He hung up the phone without letting me say anything else. I sighed. Logically I knew I didn't have to give him anything. He was a bully, and I'd had enough of him trying to capitalize on the life I had made for myself. If he actually needed my help, I would give it to him—no questions asked—but he didn't. This was all his own doing. I was not going to let his toxicity ruin my night or my good mood. No way was I going to transfer him the money he demanded.

I walked down the hallway toward the greenroom to grab some dinner. Through the propped-open door of Jamie's dressing room, I witnessed the ballet lesson he was giving Dean. Watching Dean working on his plies, I immediately felt better. It was hilarious, and I had to give both Jamie and Dean props for going through with their bet and continuing the ritual of ballet lessons every night before the show. I waved at my boyfriend— boyfriend!—and continued down the hall.

We went from Newcastle to Edinburgh to Glasgow. Up through the highlands of Scotland and then over to Belfast and Dublin. Cities and shows blended; I don't think I had ever been happier. I was with my band making the music we were born to create. Things with Jamie kept getting better with every new experience we shared. We learned each other's routines. We started doing yoga together every morning to center our bodies for the day. He told me more about himself—his time at Tisch, his tragically short dance career, his friends and colleagues from back home. I told him about my mom, all of the different bases I'd lived on growing up, and a couple of the boyfriends and girlfriends I'd had.

I got two more calls from my dad when we were in the British Isles and one from my brother Joe. All three times I let the calls go to voice mail, refusing to answer or entertain their requests. They were impatient, frustrated, and a little threatening. I deleted the messages from my phone as soon as I'd listened to them. Life was so good right now. My dad and brother were thousands of miles away, and their petty intimidation tactics had little effect on me.

The band made its way through Cork, Limerick, and finally Galway. The vibe throughout Ireland was incredible. Every crowd loved us, and every night was a party. Jamie and Hayden had been with us for a month already, and even though the original hysteria of their video had dimmed slightly, the added element of dance was a showstopper at every venue.

Dean, Ash, Carter, and I began to talk about what would come after this tour. We had agreed before it began that we wanted more time off before working on whatever was next. Carter had promised Chase they would spend the whole summer together as a reward for having been separated for so long. I didn't know exactly what I would do with so much time off, although it was nice to look forward to a break on the horizon. The next album—or tour or whatever happened—would only be seriously discussed after we all got our bearings. With the profile of the band continuing to rise, we could afford to take a little time for ourselves in a way we hadn't in the past.

We had two days off in Galway before flying over to Portugal for the next cluster of shows. On the first day, we mistakenly decided to head out as a pack to explore the city. It lasted about an hour before Carter got so helplessly mobbed that we needed to retreat back to the hotel. Eventually we were able to sneak back out to continue looking around. Even though it wasn't nearly as much fun, we thought it was best for the group to split up. Jamie and I went together. It was almost like a real date, which we hadn't really had the opportunity to do before. We wandered the streets hand in hand and largely flew under the radar.

"Oh, let's go in here," Jamie said. "I wanted to get myself a claddagh ring, and this is the original store that sells them."

"A what?" I asked.

He tugged my hand to look in a store window. It was a jewelry shop, and I tried not to overanalyze ring shopping with my boyfriend of just over a month.

"Claddagh rings. Galway's famous for them. See?"

I looked at the funny-shaped rings through the glass. There was a heart in the center, with what looked like two hands holding it and a crown on top. The store had hundreds of different models of the design, everything from plain silver to jewels of all colors. Jamie traced the outline on the poster in the window.

"The hands mean friendship, the heart's obviously love, and the crown stands for loyalty. They're hundreds of years old. Traditionally they're engagement or wedding rings, but a lot of the time now they symbolize friendship. Personally I just love the design. I read about them in a book when I was little, and I always wanted one. I'm gonna go inside. Did you want to come or… is this too weird?" Jaime asked.

His speech was fast when he was talking about weddings and engagement, almost like he'd lost sight of the meaning of the rings and was only now realizing how awkward it might come off as he was speaking about it. I laughed, trying to brush off any lingering embarrassment. He wasn't proposing or anything crazy like that. He wanted a ring for himself. Hell, he wasn't even asking me to buy it for him. It was so not a big deal. Right?

"Let's go in," I said.

I opened the door for him and immediately a young salesgirl greeted us. Jamie and I wandered, looking through the cases of claddagh rings and other Irish-themed trinkets. I wasn't someone who had ever worn jewelry of any kind. There were a couple of times I had bought a necklace or earrings for a past girlfriend, but it never would have occurred to me to buy a ring for myself simply because I wanted one. The thought made me smile. I loved how independent Jamie was. If he wanted something, he made it happen, no matter what anyone else's opinion was.

Jamie eventually decided on a simple silver band with the classic design. The salesgirl opened the showcase and pulled out the options for different sizes. He tried on a couple of different rings before selecting one that fit him best.

"So how do you wear this?" I asked. "Does the heart point toward you or away from you?"

"Aye, that's a part of the legend," the girl said coyly. Jamie blushed a little on the apples of his cheeks.

"They say that when you wear it on your right hand, if the heart points away from you, that means you're single. If the heart points toward you, you're spoken for," she explained.

I chuckled to myself, and my cheeks heated to match Jamie's. Clearly he had known that part before the girl explained it. The whole experience with the ring had been a little awkward, perhaps only because my feelings for Jamie were so strong after such a short amount of time. This shopping excursion emphasized how fast we were moving, but I had no intention of putting on the brakes if he didn't.

Jamie paid for the ring using his credit card before picking it up off the counter to slip it on his finger. He hesitated for a second, leaving the ring almost 90 degrees to his digit and tensed, knowing I was watching him.

"Allow me?" I asked him quietly, glancing at the salesgirl to make sure she was still going about her work elsewhere.

He nodded, looking me in the eye.

I took the piece of silver from him and made sure the heart was pointing toward my boyfriend before slipping it over his finger.

Definitely spoken for. He looked down at his hand and smiled.

Jamie

OUR outing into Galway had been wonderful. I got to spend the whole day with Beau window shopping and taking in the energy of the town. Until I had the bright idea to go and find myself a claddagh ring. I honestly hadn't considered about any implications before I was pulling him into the original jewelry store. As soon as I suggested it, I realized how it might come off— taking him into a ring shop after dating for a month. Fortunately, Beau had been super sweet and supportive about the whole thing, and it had barely been awkward at all.

In reciprocity, I wanted to do something special for Beau. I had never had much clout before but apparently being a part of the Inevitable Thorns tour earned me some special favors with the hotel staff.

The following day was our last in Galway. We spent the afternoon hanging out and watching Netflix together, relaxing and recharging a little. Shortly before 7:00 p.m. I suggested we go and grab some dinner. I kept the invitation as casual as possible, not wanting to alert Beau that anything was amiss.

"Where are we going?" Beau asked in the elevator when he realized we were going up instead of down.

"You'll see," I said with a wink.

The elevator door opened onto the rooftop patio, and Beau squeezed my hand as he gasped. Although it was technically closed for the winter months, I had arranged specially to have the space set up for us for a dinner date and an evening of stargazing. The rooftop had strings of lightbulbs draped around romantically. There were a couple of outdoor heaters turned on to fight off the chill. A small table for two was in the center, with silver cloches keeping the plates warm, as well as a bottle of white wine in a matching ice bucket. A cozy nest of blankets and pillows had been laid out under one of the heaters. The hotel staff had gone above and beyond. It was absolutely perfect.

"Jamie," Beau said reverently. He looked at me in a way that made me want to always protect him and keep him safe. I wanted to earn those looks forever. He snaked his arms around my back. I held him close and kissed him softly.

"Dinner?" I asked as I led him by the small of his back over to the table. I pulled out his chair, got him situated, and then went to take my seat.

"Jamie, this is—" Beau started again, not making much more progress on his sentence the second time.

"I wanted a night for us." I shrugged, downplaying the whole event.

While I didn't have a huge amount of experience being a boyfriend, I guess I was somewhat of a romantic at heart. The look on Beau's face in the Irish moonlight was all I needed to be convinced I had done the right thing. My little rock star liked the romance too, as it turned out.

We laughed together as I struggled with the cork on the bottle, eventually getting it open but making a bit of a mess. I licked some of the spilled liquid from my fingers and enjoyed how Beau's eyes darkened with the appearance of my tongue. He poured us each some wine, and we clinked our glasses in a toast before digging into our meals.

Long after dinner was done, we lingered at the table, chatting and flirting. Eventually the temperature dropped, and we moved to the nest of blankets. There was a little plate of chocolate-dipped strawberries for dessert, which was a delicious treat. Beau leaned against me as he licked an errant drop of melted chocolate off my bottom lip. While it was cozy under the heat lamps, I was happy to have my boyfriend to keep me warm. I gazed upward.

"Tell me about the stars," I said.

Beau sighed peacefully and gazed upward for a moment. He leaned as close to my line of vision as possible and pointed up.

"Do you see those three bright ones in a row?"

I squinted my eyes, nodding when I saw where he was gesturing.

"That's Orion's belt. You can see almost an hourglass shape with those three in the middle? That makes up the rest of the Orion constellation. It's got some of the brightest stars in the sky. Because it's so recognizable, almost every ancient civilization had a myth created about it. The Egyptians associated Orion with Osiris, the god of rebirth. The Aztecs used it as part of a ritual they performed to postpone the end of the world. The Greeks said that Orion was a superhuman hunter, the son of Poseidon. I kind of love that everyone on Earth sees the same stars, but we all see them differently. We give them our own meaning. It's symbolic of everything, really."

"That's beautiful," I said.

I kissed Beau's temple and looked up into the sky as he told me more about all the shapes and patterns he knew. The vastness of the sky and the universe seemed to swallow us up until all that existed was his voice and the abstract warmth of his body next to me. Sometimes I saw the constellation he depicted, and sometimes I couldn't make them out, but hearing Beau talk so passionately was more important than understanding every word.

After the cold had seeped into our bones beyond the help of the blankets and heaters, we made our way back down to his room. It had been a night unrivaled by any I could remember. "Galaxies" had brought Beau and I together in the first place, so it only made sense that looking at the stars was the backdrop for the moment when I fell in love with him.

Beau

"**BEAU.** Beau, wake up."

The pleasant haze of slumber fell away with Jamie shaking me and calling my name. I had been in the middle of a dream—one that I could no longer remember—and my mind was slow and groggy. Pulling the blankets up over my head, I tried to hide from the inevitable start of the day. We were flying to Porto, Portugal, this afternoon. No way had I slept that late, and if there had been an actual danger of missing the flight, Cory would be pounding at the door, berating my ass.

"Beau, I'm not kidding. We have a situation."

I grumbled as I tossed the blankets off my head. I was assaulted by the bright blue light of Jamie's phone, which he was holding up to my face. After I rubbed my eyes, the image on the screen came into focus. It was a grainy photo taken through glass and from a distance, but it definitely showed me putting the claddagh ring on Jamie's finger in the jewelry store. We were facing each other, frozen midlaugh. The frame captured the distinct color of Jamie's hair and enough of my face to make it basically undeniable that it was us in the photo.

"It's all over Twitter. Retweeted hundreds of times. Tagging Thorns and both of our personal accounts. Saying, well, I'm sure you can guess what they're saying."

Jamie's voice had an edge, sounding high and panicky. His leg was jiggling and shaking the bed, making me slightly nauseous. I put my hand on his leg to still it. Letting out a sigh, I surprised myself with how calm I was about this huge invasion of our privacy.

"I'm so sorry, Beau. I wasn't thinking," Jamie said quietly.

I kissed his tense lips to try to assure him I wasn't mad at him.

"It's not your fault," I said. "Something like this was bound to happen eventually."

Taking Jamie's phone, I scrolled through a couple of dumb comments. There were a range of judgments, remarks on my sexuality, and congratulations on our "engagement." I snorted at the implication and put the device facedown on the bedside table. With my arms wrapped around Jamie, I tucked my face into the crook of his neck.

"It was my stupid idea to go into that shop," Jamie said.

He was so upset with himself. I wasn't sure how to reassure him that there was no way I would be angry about his part in this.

"The location sensationalized what would have happened regardless of where we were. Any moron should notice that the photo was flipped and it's actually your right hand the ring is on. The text on the signs is all backward."

"Should we say something? People are making a big deal out of not knowing you were into guys."

"It doesn't bug me that people know I'm bi," I said honestly. "It's never been about that. It's just that it's a violation. I make music. There's this bizarre assumption that being a musician equates to fans feeling entitled to know everything about my life. Or even worse, thinking they deserve to have an opinion on it."

I picked up Jamie's phone again, scrolling back to the comment that had really pissed me off.

"Like this asshole. How could anyone possibly think you're 'not good enough' to be with me? That fucking sucks, you know?"

Agitated, I scrubbed my hands over my face. Jamie gently took my hand in his and kissed it. His eyes were gentle and warm.

"They're jealous," he said. "Your fans love you."

"It's rude. Creepy and rude."

I was getting worked up now. Far more than when I had seen the photos to begin with. Everybody who'd ever met Jamie would know he was far too good for me, not the other way around. He was kind and caring—as proven by our stargazing dinner date last night. He was independent and passionate and crazy talented. Not to mention he was sexy as hell and gave me exactly what I needed in bed—not that I would be sharing that last point with anyone.

"We should get up," Jamie said into my hair a few minutes later. "Do you wanna grab a shower while I order some food? We've got another hour before we need to head to the airport."

I nodded. I wished we could share a shower, but from past experience I was fully aware that would end up taking more time than we had.

"Come on, rock star, Jamie said, pulling me up when I didn't make any effort to move. "Let's face the music."

Beau

WHEN we landed in Porto, things had gotten worse instead of better.

After deplaning we were whisked through the jet bridge ahead of everyone else on board. It was a small airport, and the goal in these situations was always to travel as a pack and move as quickly as possible until we could get out of the public part of the airport. Taking private flights was not always in the budget, as much as we wished it could be. Jamie and Dean were in the lead—chatting and laughing about something or other—with us all attempting to keep Carter as concealed as possible in the middle of the group. At least that was the plan until I spotted something out of the corner of my eye and stopped short.

"*Oof*," Cory said, walking into me as I froze unexpectedly.

I moved out of step from the rest of our unit, staring at the TV screen up above one of the central rows of seats. It was one of those trashy celebrity gossip shows, with a host who looked like she had undergone so much Botox treatment she could hardly move her face. Her bubblegum-pink dress was low cut, and her tits were pushed up to her chin.

The host wasn't what caught my eye, however. It was the interviewee who sat across from her who I focused on.

My father.

He was wearing a pinstripe suit with a white shirt. It was in better shape than any of the clothes I had seen him in, with the exception of his military uniforms. Not a food stain or a wrinkle in sight. He was even wearing a fucking tie. His eyes looked focused—almost sharp—and certainly not lazy with booze like they had in December. His back was stiff, his whole demeanor overly posed, and he was on his best behavior. His name was displayed proudly in bold text across the screen below him.

I stood there, mouth gaping open, unable to look away. A split-screen image appeared with the photo Jamie had shown me earlier featuring the two of us in the jewelry store. A headline below read "Beau Davis of Inevitable Thorns Engaged to Male Backup Dancer!"

"Beau, what the hell are you doing! Come on." Cory appeared next to me and tugged on my jacket. He followed my gaze upward to the screen.

Oh God.

"Yes, Janet, we knew he was secretly gay, but I didn't know he was gay for this Jamie guy specifically," my dad said on screen. His thick caterpillar eyebrows were raised, and he was doing his best to make himself look like the reliable victim. It was an act I knew well.

"The fuck?" Cory said, mirroring my own reaction.

"I mean, Beau's a good kid, but it's not the first time he's made a quick decision for some tail, if you know what I mean." My dad snorted at what he probably considered to be a joke. Tits McReporter laughed along with him before asking another question I didn't hear.

I choked a little, sickened by what I was seeing. The crass language, the misinformation. I felt queasy. My legs were weak and threatened to give out. The blood pounded in my head, and I pinched the bridge of my nose, desperate to make the whole scene disappear. I couldn't think, couldn't process what was going on.

"Beau?" Jamie suddenly materialized beside me. His voice sounded muffled to my ears as his arm snaked around my waist, stopping me from toppling over.

"Oh fuck," he muttered under his breath.

"I always thought he was doing the singer, to be honest. Maybe that's going on as well." My dad thoughtfully stroked his chin. The act was appalling and disgusting, intended to spread gossip and hurt.

I heard Carter scoff somewhere behind me. Was everyone here? I tried to focus, but nothing was penetrating; tried to stand on my own without Jamie's assistance, but I was too weak. Nothing made sense. My head was spinning.

"I dunno if I'd stop them getting hitched. Can't say I agree with it, but not my place to stop it. Better sign a damn prenup, though, if he's smart. Only one type of dancing I know pays the bills. Hell, maybe he is that kinda dancer. Who knows where this guy came from?"

"Okay, that's enough," Cory said, taking control of the situation. He sounded far away even though it looked like he was standing next to me. Cory pulled out his cell phone. "Beau, you don't need to watch this crap. Let's go. This will go away."

No it wouldn't. Not really, anyway.

Cory started to move the whole exhibition along. I was vaguely aware that we were still in a public airport, and we were beginning to get some curious stares. Jamie kept his arm tight around me, guiding and protecting me. I stared at Jamie and tried to thank him, but the words got stuck before they could come out.

I put one foot in front of the other mechanically until we were whisked into a waiting SUV.

Jamie

THAT fucking bastard. How dare he?

How dare he go on some scuzzy gossip program and talk about Beau like that. Talk about *his son* like that. Talk about me and Carter and God knows whatever other bullshit came flying out of his boorish mouth. His words were insulting, ignorant, and downright homophobic.

I heard the water shut off and stopped pacing long enough to move into the bathroom to check on Beau. Immediately a cloud of steam hit me as I opened the door. I grabbed one of the oversized, fluffy white bath towels off the warming rack. Beau stepped out from behind the glass wall, his skin red and his hair dripping.

"Hey, that feel any better?" I asked, wrapping the towel around his naked body and rubbing the dampness from him. Beau shot me a weak attempt at a smile, but it didn't reach his eyes.

"A little," he said, but I could tell he was lying.

He picked some pajama pants out of his suitcase and pulled them on. Beau made his way over to the bed and lay back on the luxurious sheets. I joined him, dragging his body closer to me. He was rigid with tension. I clicked on the TV to look for something mindless to watch.

Of course the flat screen blared to life on an entertainment show that was talking about us. Beau froze against me, and I mentally cursed myself. I tried to change the channel quickly but got messed up by the unfamiliar remote.

"Fuck," I said as I fought to switch the station, eventually figuring out how to turn the bloody thing off.

"It's okay," he mumbled, staring blankly at the black screen.

I rubbed my face and sighed. "I'm sorry. I should have known that would happen."

Beau had been barely functioning since he caught sight of the interview back in the airport. I was out of my depth here. He kept pulling away from me, and he had barely spoken a word. I hated that I felt so helpless. I kissed his temple, not knowing what else to do. He recoiled a little, which threw me off. I took a breath and pulled back to give him some room.

"Why would he do that?" I asked, genuinely confused. "I know you said your relationship isn't great, but was he really so desperate to get his fifteen minutes of fame that he would sell you out like that?"

Beau shook his head. "He did it for the money."

The pieces spun together in my head. Of course. Beau had mentioned his dad and brother taking advantage of his padded bank account in the past. The reasoning made the whole thing more disgusting. Not only did Beau's dad completely use him to get a payday, but he sensationalized the situation and said horrible things in the process. Probably to land himself more follow-up interviews. Ugh. An abhorrent feeling washed over my skin.

"Oh, Beau, that's horrible. That's so much worse."

He made a low sound of agreement in his throat. A silence fell between the two of us. He was right next to me, but he felt a million miles away.

"I think I need some time tonight," Beau said slowly, as if he was formulating the words as he went. "To process all of this. Alone."

Alone.

His request hit me like a kick to the stomach. He sat up, shifting away from me as I lay there frozen in place. I stared at him, the unexpected, hurtful words sinking in more with each heartbeat.

Alone.

My eyes started to sting and I squeezed them closed. Bile rose in my throat. Even with him pulling away, it never occurred that he wouldn't want me around at all. I thought we were on the same page. That we were in this horrible situation together and we would deal with it as a couple. Beau wanted to be by himself.

When my lungs began to burn—demanding oxygen—I drew in a shaky breath.

"I want… I want to help," I said, upset with how wobbly my voice was.

I fought for control. Beau touched my arm, and I forced myself to look at him. His brown eyes were filled with pain. He might be saying that he wanted to be alone, but his eyes told another story. He needed me to stick by his side.

"I know," he said gently. "And I appreciate that. This thing with my dad, it's complicated. I want to talk to you, explain it all. I just need a few hours to figure it out in my head first. Please, Jamie?"

Please.

A second ago I thought the word "alone" had stung. But this new word *shattered* me.

How many times had he said that word to me before? Begging me to touch him. Begging me to let him come.

This time he was begging me to go away.

He knew I had no willpower when he used that word with me. I didn't know what else to do. So I did what he asked. I left.

I packed up my hurt along with my bags, and I left.

Jamie

THIRTY minutes after leaving Beau's suite, I was sitting at the hotel bar by myself. My bags were upstairs in the single hotel room I was guaranteed as part of my contract; a room I hadn't exercised the use of since I had joined the tour.

The first vodka soda had slipped down my throat so easily I was already working on my second. I was such a lightweight that my head was starting to spin, thanks to the booze. At least it was better than the spinning thanks to my conversation with Beau.

My conversation with Beau? My fight with Beau?

Did that count as a fight? I may have been fighting for us, but he certainly wasn't fighting for me, that was for damn sure.

The barstool next to me squeaked as it was pulled out. I looked up from my drink to find Dean next to me with a beer in hand.

"Can you go sit over there?" Dean asked, pointing to the end of the empty bar.

I stared at him, my head cloudy and working slowly.

"Come on!" he prompted. "Then I can walk over to your sad-sack face and be all 'nobody puts Baby in a corner.' But I can't do that here because you're in the middle of the room."

I snorted, the closest I could give to a reaction right now. Dean laughed at his own joke anyway. His ridiculousness cracked my mood a little; my new friend never took anything too seriously.

We sat for a few long moments in silence. It was nice. Some of the tension rolled off my shoulders. Dean let me work through it, yet eventually I caved.

"I thought you were always Baby?" I fought a smile.

"You look like you need it more tonight," Dean said. "Everything okay, Jam-Jam?" He raised his eyebrows, looking more sincere than I'd ever seen him.

"I dunno." I sighed. "This bullshit with Beau's dad's really bugging him. He didn't want to be a headline, and it's my fault he's become one. Now all this crap is happening as a result. I feel awful about it, but I'm not sure how to help when he's pushing me away."

My voice cracked and the words started coming out faster. "He wanted to be alone tonight. I tried to help but I made it worse. I think he's going to end it."

Dean stood up and gestured for me to copy him. He pulled me into his arms and hugged me as I quietly broke down.

"I'm sorry." I sniffled as we both sat again. He took a drink and I tried to inconspicuously wipe the moisture from my eyes. It was probably a lost cause, but whatever.

"Jam-Jam, I've known Beau for a long time. A looong time. He hasn't had the easiest go of it. His mom died when he was young. His dad... well you got the gist of him today. He was in love with Cart for, like, ever. He'll deny that if you ask him, but even *I* could fucking tell."

Dean snickered and rolled his eyes. He was making a list on his fingers of every point he added. I wasn't sure where he was going with this or how it was supposed to make me feel better.

He carried on. "His brother's a pompous ass. The 'Galaxies' guy treated him like shit—"

"What's your point, Dean?" I cut him off, not wanting to hear the nitty-gritty of my boyfriend's past lovers from someone other than him.

"My point, Ginger Jam, is that Beau's used to people leaving. He's *not used* to you being there for him. Give him time. He's happier with you than he's ever been. He'll come around."

Dean swallowed the last mouthful of his beer. He tossed a fifty on the bar before clapping my shoulder and pulling my vodka glass away from me.

"And drink some water. Cory will kick your ass if you show up hungover tomorrow. Trust me on that." He winked before heading back into the hotel lobby and toward the elevators.

I watched him walk away until he was out of sight. My shoulders sagged and I breathed deeply.

Dean's pep talk had helped a lot. He had known Beau far longer than I had. That must be worth something. I felt so guilty for inadvertently compromising the privacy Beau valued so much. Beau had seemed relatively blasé when I had shown him the leaked photos of us this morning. It wasn't until he had seen his dad on the talk show that he'd broken down. That gave me some comfort that it wasn't actually me he was upset with.

It just sucked that he had shut me out. It felt like the morning after the *Grammys* when Beau had left and I had woken up alone. Only back then I was just a hookup. We had come so far since that. I wanted him to talk to me when he was so visibly upset. I wanted to help and support him, unlike the others who had disappeared. I wanted a say, dammit!

If Beau needed space, I would give it to him. I would be patient and wait for him to come to me. But there was no way I was letting him walk away for good without having any input.

Beau

THE hurt in Jamie's eyes when I told him I wanted to be alone made me want to snatch back the words immediately. I hated that I had done that to him. Hated that I had pushed him away after he had been nothing but supportive.

It had been three days since we had spoken. He'd been avoiding me at the theaters, only coming out of his dressing room for his ballet lessons with Dean and when he was needed onstage for "Galaxies." Most nights he left before the end of the show and took a cab back to the hotel. Cory automatically gave him keycards for his own room now. It was agony to be so close to him yet so far away.

Every time I stepped outside, I had cameras in my face. For the past couple of years, we'd had to deal with paparazzi every so often, but the obnoxious fuckers were following me everywhere these days. They said horrible things to me—intended to generate a reaction—that were hard enough not to respond to. When they asked where Jamie was, all I wanted to do was hide and cry.

I yearned to tell Jamie I was sorry. That I was wrong for thinking I needed to handle things on my own. That a secure relationship with a reliable partner was new for me. That disappointing him felt worse than anything my dad had done. The longer the silence went on, the harder it became to find the words to fix it. Harder to tell if he *wanted me* to fix it.

I held no animosity toward Jamie for the photo in Galway or for anything that had happened as a result. It was as much my fault as it was his. My dad's publicity stunt, on the other hand, was unforgivable. He knew how much I hated having the media poking into my private business, and he'd exploited it for revenge and for his own financial gain. I needed some time to straighten it out in my head, but I knew I didn't want to have a relationship with my dad or Joe anymore. Since my mom died, there had always been a certain amount of guilt pushing me to be loyal to the few family members I had left. Not anymore. My dad had caused too much destruction and hurt to those who I actually cared about. I was completely done this time.

Whenever I passed Jamie backstage and he avoided eye contact, my heart broke a little more. It felt like I was losing him—if I hadn't lost him already. Jamie had been so incredibly supportive that night. Why the hell would he want to be in a relationship with someone who treated him like shit when he was only trying to help?

"Galaxies" was the biggest torture. Jamie was so damn beautiful on that stage. It was impossible not to be mesmerized. He was always self-conscious about his body and his performance, but he took my breath away every single night. When I had first encountered him in the studio at Juilliard so many months ago, I saw right away that he was a phenomenal dancer. Now that I knew *him*—his drive, his compassion, his thoughtfulness about his choreography—I recognized that his talents were limitless. He was just beginning the journey of his career and he was bound to create groundbreaking pieces at every turn.

I must have been a masochist because after the show one night, even though I was exhausted, I stayed behind and watched from the wings as Jamie and Hayden went through a few things by themselves on stage. Seeing Jamie rolling around practically naked with the guy who was playing the part of my verbally abusive ex was horrible beyond words. Jamie was portraying me, clinging to a former lover when the real-life version of me was holding on to him by my fingernails. It was all a little too poignant right now. Like the song, I had no idea what the ending would be; only this time, I desperately wanted a specific outcome.

Why had I fucked this up so badly?

Carter walked up to me, following my sightline.

"Talk to him," Carter commanded gently.

"I'm not sure how," I said. "He's so upset that I asked him to go. He won't even look at me. I'm not ready for this to be over. I love him."

"Even more of a reason to talk to him." Carter chuckled. "Listen, if I've learned anything over the past year from being with Chase, it's that it's really easy to make stupid assumptions when you're hurt or mad. But when you actually discuss what's going on, it's rarely as bad as you make it out to be in your head. You've always needed to handle decisions on your own. Jamie *wants* to be there for you. Apologize to him and let him help."

I nodded to Carter. Of course he was right. I needed to suck up my damn pride and see if Jamie would forgive me for not having a damn clue about what I was doing.

My phone started to ring in my pocket. I scooped it out and frowned when I saw the ID on my call display. Carter stalled beside me as I flashed him the name on the screen.

"You know, you don't need to answer it," he told me.

I sighed. "This is going to happen sometime. I might as well get it over with."

While I was still working up the nerve to talk to Jamie, this call had been a long time coming and I was ready to get it over with. To be done with my dad for good.

After one last glance at my beautiful dancer, I left the wings for the backstage hallway and closed the door behind me. I swiped the screen to answer the call.

"Dad," I answered tersely without a salutation.

"Fuck you! Fuck you, fuck you, fuck you, you dirty asslicker," my lovely father yelled into the phone the moment I picked up. His words were slurred—surprise, surprise. I held the phone away from my ear and turned down the volume, fighting the urge to hang up. He would only call me back repeatedly anyway.

"How the fuck are *you* possibly mad at *me*?"

"You're tryin' ta bank—" His word was cut off by a loud hiccup, "—bankrupt my ass, you lil shit."

I took a breath, willing myself to stay composed.

Nope, not going to work this time.

"How the fuck am I doing that, Dad?" I practically snarled at him. "By not giving you money? Newsflash, you have a damn job. You and Joe both do in fact. The choice you make to piss your money away does not mean I'm bankrupting you."

The door behind me opened, and Jamie appeared, sweat fresh on his skin and concern written on his face. The whole building had probably overheard me yelling. Jamie closed the door and took a step or two toward me until he stood beside me for the first time in days, looking slightly unsure but not seeming likely to bolt.

"By fuckin' servin' me with goddam papers suin' me for defam… defam… ation," my dad finally got out through the hiccups.

I narrowed my eyes, wondering what the hell he was talking about. While I generally didn't believe a word that came out of my dad's mouth, this didn't seem like something he would concoct out of thin air. At that moment, I caught sight of Cory down the hall, talking away on his own cell phone. The visual triggered a memory. Cory. His words from the airport came back to me.

This will go away.

I smiled to myself, realizing what had probably happened. The poison my dad had spewed would surely not be appreciated by Cory or his bosses. We were one of the biggest bands on their label, and it made sense that they would want to protect us from bullies and slander in the media.

"Well, what did you expect to happen, Dad? You can't go on TV and say whatever you want. That shit you said hurt. It hurt me and my bandmates and my boyfriend."

I risked looking up at Jamie. His eyes were soft and vulnerable at my words. God, I hoped that label was still true. I slowly reached for his hand, scared to make a wrong move but suddenly needing his steadfast support. He gazed down at our joined fingers before his eyes locked with mine. A tentative smile brushed his lips, encouraging me to go on without needing to say anything. The interaction gave me a rush of confidence.

My dad continued, his words mattering even less than they had a minute ago now that I had Jamie's hand in mine. "He's usin' you, Beau. Jus' like all th'others. Don't be naïve. He only wants your money. Then he'll dump your sad ass."

"Sounds fucking familiar, doesn't it? I tell you what, Dad, Jamie's not like that. Not like you. He's loyal and kind. He wants what's best for me and is there when shit hits the fan. He works hard for what he has, and he pays his own way. There's only two people I know who try to take advantage of my money, and they both live under your roof. Leave me alone, leave my band alone, and leave Jamie the fuck alone."

I hung up the phone before he had a chance to respond.

Jamie let out a slow breath and flashed me a shy smile. How had I ever thought dealing with this on my own was better than with his support? All he'd done was stand there next to me and hold my fucking hand, and it felt like I could do anything. Yes, I had started the conversation with my dad by myself, but it was Jamie who gave me the courage to finally hang up the phone.

Now that was done, I desperately wanted to talk to Jamie. To apologize over and over and beg him to give me another chance. And I would. But I wanted time to settle things with Jamie properly, and there was one other piece of business that needed addressing first.

I gestured for him to come with me and we walked hand in hand down the hall to where Cory was standing.

Shoulders back and chest out, I waited for Cory to end his call, which he did quickly when he noticed my presence. Honestly I didn't know what to feel. I disagreed wholeheartedly with my father taking the interview and saying what he did; there was no defending him, and it made my relationship with him simple. He could not be trusted, and I wanted him out of my life completely. I also fucking *hated* that Cory had started legal proceedings against a member of my family without my knowledge or permission. The sentiment was appreciated—and ultimately I probably would have agreed to it—but to go behind my back and sue my dad was a big decision that I should have been consulted on.

"You can't just do that, Core. Don't you think you should have told me you were suing my father?"

Jamie's eyes went wide beside me. He had heard most of my end of the conversation with my dad, but evidently not the important bits. Cory extended his hands, palms up in a defensive stance.

"We couldn't not, Beau. It was too big a liability to have him spouting bullshit like that. I saw what it did to you. Thank God we didn't have a show that night. You were a mess. Saying that shit about Carter's relationship or Jamie's work history? It was negative press that was inaccurate and harmful to the brand."

"I know that. Obviously I'm not defending him. But you could have given me a fucking heads-up that you were serving him fucking papers today!"

My jaw clenched tightly and my hands balled into fists at my sides. This whole thing was one hit after another. The photo. The interview. The lawsuit. I was just beginning to feel better about one aspect of this mess when I got blindsided by the next thing. It was all such crap, stemming from a stolen photo of what was a benign, happy moment. The entire incident was one invasion of privacy after another, and it *sucked* having no say or control of any of it. When the hell was my turn to set the record straight?

Oh. I paused in thought. Maybe that was it. The thought of giving a solo interview or making a public statement about my love life made me want to break out in hives, but maybe that was the best option here. Give Beau a chance to speak up for himself for once, huh? A foreign fucking concept.

"How is that even possible to sue someone without knowing about it?" Jamie asked.

"The record company sued for defamation. It's not in Beau's name. The label is suing on behalf of the band," Cory explained. "Look, Beau, we didn't want to start a war here, but we can't have him saying that shit. We could have put a lot more zeros on the suit, but we kept it at a little over what he would have been paid for the interview and stipulated that he's not to speak about any member of the Thorns, or the band itself, publicly."

I gritted my teeth. "Again I'm not pissed that you did it. I'm pissed that you didn't *tell me*. I have no control here, Cory. All I want is to feel like I have a say. Like *we*—" I gestured between myself and Jamie. "—have a say."

"I get that, Beau. For what it's worth, I'm sorry. Did you want me to talk to the label about dropping the suit?"

I thought about it for a second.

"Try to settle for what he got from the interview," I conceded. "He doesn't have any money besides that. And donate it to charity—it's blood money. Also I want an interview. Soon, before I think about it too much. Give it to whoever you think would be good and not make too big of a thing of it. I want to set the record straight. Officially come out, or whatever. Talk about the song. Our relationship—if Jamie's okay with that part of it. I'll do it once, and then I want to go back to not being a fucking headline."

I looked over at Jamie, who took a deep breath and nodded. He gave me a soft smile, reassuring me silently that he was okay with whatever I needed to do.

"I'll make it happen," Cory said.

He headed off in the direction of the production office, leaving Jamie and me by ourselves in the deserted hallway.

"Are you okay?" Jamie asked tentatively once we were alone.

While I'd felt brave on the call and with Cory, now that the adrenaline was wearing off, I was exhausted. I looked up at the beautiful man in front of me, and my vision started to blur as I fought back tears. People in my life had a habit of leaving, but Jamie rushed to my side when I was upset even after I had been so awful to him.

He wrapped me up in his arms and held me, whispering that he was proud of me over and over again into my ear. I clung to him as he rubbed soothing patterns down my spine.

"I'm so sorry, Jamie," I said.

"It's okay, I know. I know," he murmured into my hair.

The muscles in my back eventually relaxed with his touch. God, I wanted to live in his strong embrace forever.

"Can we go back to the hotel and talk some more?" I asked nervously.

"Of course. There's nowhere else I would rather be."

Jamie

BACK at the hotel, Beau and I were lounging around in his room—which was probably *our* room again—sharing a post-show pizza. We were back on an even footing, or at least we were heading in that direction. He had apologized repeatedly in the cab, explaining some more of the backstory with his dad and why he had shut down so hard when he saw the interview.

Even with the lack of meat the pizza hit the spot. The two of us ate in silence until the pie was almost gone. Refueling helped my mentality, and I hoped the food was having the same effect on Beau.

"So. Where do we go from here?" I finally asked.

Beau's eyes went wide, and his jaw slackened a little.

"Like?" He gestured with his finger between both of our chests. "I still want... do you not?"

"Oh God, yes. Yes." I reached out hastily to grab his leg, not wanting my words to be misinterpreted. I absolutely did not want to end things between us over all the stupid from the last few days. "I want to be with you, Beau. This is new for both of us. We're figuring it out together. But I want to go back to how things were before."

His shoulders released some of the tension and panic they had been holding. "It's a lot, you know? I wouldn't blame you if you didn't want to. I was so selfish when you were only trying to help. And my dad. He said such horrible things about you."

I cleared the pizza box from the bed, giving myself a moment to choose my words carefully. Beau was still fragile right now, and I wanted to help, not inadvertently make the situation worse. I sat cross-legged on the bed and took his hands in mine.

"What he said is *not* your fault, rock star. You know that, right?"

Beau hesitated but eventually nodded. "I know."

"Even though you didn't give him money, this is not your fault. He wasn't right about you, and he sure as hell wasn't right about me."

"I know," Beau said, slightly more confidently this time with a ghost of a smile.

"And as for us, we need to talk to each other. I can't help if you don't let me. You wanting to be alone hurt. I didn't know if you blamed me or if I had done something wrong. But I get it. Just please don't shut me out next time."

"You're right. I'm sorry. I'm not used to having someone to rely on. A partner. For what it's worth, I wasn't trying to push you away. I just needed a little time to think. But I handled it wrong."

He purposely skimmed the piece of silver on my finger that started all the drama. I still wore it pointing toward myself, my heart knowing we remained a couple even when my head questioned us. He trembled slightly as I ran my thumb over his jaw. Slowly, deliberately, I leaned in, pausing a breath away so he could stop me if he wanted to. Beau closed the final gap between us, touching his soft lips to mine. Nothing had ever felt so right in my life.

"We good, rock star?" I asked.

"We're good," he confirmed.

I kissed him again and enjoyed the simple contact after going without for so long. He smiled at me genuinely.

Tired of the heaviness of the last few days, I gambled on a joke to lighten the mood.

"He called me a stripper," I deadpanned with a raised eyebrow.

Finally Beau chuckled. I reveled in the sound.

"I've heard that's where the money is," Beau joked back slowly, repeating his father's words in jest.

I burst out laughing. "Oh really?" I challenged.

"Yup, I—"

I cut him off before he could continue, pouncing on him as he yelped in protest. We play-wrestled on the bed, struggling for power and trying to pin each other down. He was a squirmy little bastard when he wanted to be. Beau pulled out the big guns and started tickling my sides, mercilessly exploiting my weaknesses. It felt indescribably good to have fun with him again. Beau sat on my hips as I struggled beneath him, trying to regain my breath from the ongoing tickle-assault.

Despite the discomfort, it was hard to want to win when he was straddling my lap and smiling so big. Until the trash talking started.

Eventually I'd had enough and took control again, hoisting him onto his back and using my weight to hold him down, pinning his arms over his head. He wriggled beneath me, fighting to break free. Nope! Not gonna happen, rock star.

"Give?" I asked him, wheezing.

"Never!"

He was all talk. I rolled my eyes at him, both of us knowing he didn't stand a chance if I really wanted to win. Changing position slightly, I tested a theory by pushing my thigh gently between his legs. His resulting moan and the steel length I felt through his jeans made it pretty clear my hypothesis was correct.

I ground my hips down into him, adjusting tactics.

"Oh fuck," Beau said.

He stopped grappling and his body went still immediately. I smiled, egotistically patting myself on the back for the big win. Dropping down on my elbows, I licked up the side of Beau's neck.

"Now do you give?" I whispered in his ear.

He laughed. "You're pure evil."

"Care to make things interesting?" I raised my eyebrow at him before scanning around the room for the items I was looking for. "Come over here."

I borrowed the chair that was neatly put away under the desk and spun it around. Beau took a seat, his eyes dark and intrigued. I had a feeling that taking Beau out of his own head and giving him something else to focus on was exactly what he needed tonight. Finding the long plaid scarf I had been wearing earlier in the day, I smoothed the soft fabric between my fingers.

Beau made a sound in his throat, his stare never leaving the material.

"You can tell me to stop at any time," I assured him before tying his wrists together loosely behind the chair. We had spent enough time together that I knew Beau wouldn't move if I told him to stay put, so I didn't bother securing him too tightly. It was more the mentality of being bound that would do the trick. This was going to be fun.

Finding the song I was looking for on Spotify, I cranked the bass before putting my phone on the desk next to Beau. I started moving my hips a little to the beat before meeting his lusty gaze and slowly undoing the top button on my shirt.

"Now, someone mentioned something about a stripper."

Jamie

A FEW days later, I sat in the greenroom of some reputable talk show watching Beau from a monitor. He was doing so well—poised and professional—even though I knew he'd been a nervous wreck before. Beau was through the basic small talk and was getting into the deeper questions of the interview. The first full segment was only him, as it should be. The plan was for me to join him at the end and answer a few questions about our relationship.

And reassure the world that I was *not*, in fact, a stripper.

Quite possibly the best—and certainly the most surprising—thing to come out of this whole situation was an email I received yesterday from Coleman Hale. When I had seen his name pop up in my inbox I couldn't help but roll my eyes, sure he was getting some sort of sick enjoyment out of the ordeal. In reality, the email depicted the opposite. It was a peace offering of sorts. While he hadn't changed his tune about my style of choreography, he admitted that I did it well and that the "Galaxies" piece was well constructed. The praise wasn't over-the-top like I had been hearing from other choreographers, but from him it felt like a beam of sunshine on a cloudy day.

Coleman went on to speak from his own experience about negative press making him question his artistic choices and encouraged me to focus on the people and art that mattered. It seemed we had come full circle from the horrible costume-switching disaster when we first met.

I emailed him back, thanking him and extending an olive branch of my own. Coleman and I were never going to see eye-to-eye or become best friends. However, his gesture meant a lot. The dance community was small, and I appreciated that, despite our history, Coleman knew Beau's dad was lying about me. I hoped that Coleman and I could be more civil in the future and focus on what was best for our students.

"So, Beau, we've heard a lot about you lately," the interviewer continued on the TV monitor. "As someone who makes a point to stay out of the media, this all must be a little overwhelming. To begin with, can you explain a little about the photo we've all seen now of you and Jamie Griffin in the ring store?"

A giant version of the now-infamous photo in Galway filled the screen. The live audience let out a collective "aww" as the shot zoomed in on our faces and his hands pushing the ring onto my finger.

As the photo faded back to Beau's image in the studio, the blush on his cheeks was obvious. It was endearing. He rubbed the back of his neck like there was tension there before he began to speak.

"Come on, rock star." I cheered him on, muttering under my breath. "You can do this."

"Well, Francesca, it's unfortunately not what you all think it is," he said with a charming smile. "The band was in Galway, Ireland, and they're famous for these things called claddagh rings. Maybe some of you have heard of them? I hadn't until Jamie told me. Anyway, we had the afternoon to ourselves, and Jamie had read about them when he was young and wanted one. We found this lovely little shop, and he picked a ring out and bought it for himself. It's actually one of my favorite things about Jamie; if he wants something, he does it. So if you look carefully at the text in the signage, it's all backward. The photo was flipped so it looks like it's Jamie's left hand, but it's actually his right that he wears the ring on. Sorry to disappoint everyone, but nope, we're not engaged." Beau bent his elbows and held his palms facing up in a classic "don't be mad" gesture. The audience reacted with light applause and some chatter.

I breathed a sigh of relief at Beau's well-described version of the story. I really liked that he hadn't mentioned the bit about debating which way the ring should be facing and when he essentially claimed me—it was good to keep some things for ourselves.

"But you are together?" Francesca prodded.

"Yes. I identify as bisexual. It's not a new thing for me or anything I was ever hiding. I make an effort to keep some parts of myself private, and this is one of them. It's not because I don't love our fans, but it's important to me to protect who I'm with from getting pulled into the fray, whether that's a woman or a man."

Francesca tilted her head and nodded as if she understood exactly what Beau went through.

"Jamie and I met in a cute way, actually," Beau went on. "I was helping out a friend by giving a guest lecture at his college. I got turned around trying to find the exit, and I heard our song 'Galaxies' coming from down the hall. When I found the dance studio the music was coming from, there was this beautiful man dancing by himself. He's had me wrapped around his little finger ever since."

Beau's version of our story had me smiling even though I'd heard it a couple of times before. Francesca held her hand to her heart at Beau's words.

"That's so sweet. We're going to bring Jamie out shortly. In the meantime, Beau, how are things going on the tour so far? It seems like the most recent Inevitable Thorns album has spoken to a lot of people."

Beau went on to answer the question and then a couple that followed. They were all standard interviewy things and took some of the focus away from the photo and his dad's spectacle. That was one thing Beau had made clear in his preshow chat with Francesca: he didn't want to give more power to his dad by spending too much time on the topic or stirring up more drama. I was so impressed with how Beau handled himself. He said he hated this kind of thing, yet he was funny and charming up there. He got his point across without directly calling out his dad.

The segment went to a commercial break, and a PA came to bring me out to the soundstage. Beau stood up from the couch when he noticed me.

"You did so good," I said and kissed him quickly. He grinned at me, and all the stress from the last few days seemed to fade into the background.

We got comfortable on the couch together as the technicians wired me up with a lapel microphone. How had this become my life? Beau squeezed my hand reassuringly as I guess I must have appeared a little overwhelmed looking up at all the camera gear and people staring at me.

"Ready for this?" He murmured, barely moving his lips so only I could hear.

"Ready as I'll ever be."

Francesca got back into position on the seat opposite ours and flashed a quick thumbs-up to the producer. He nodded and started counting down.

"And we're back in five, four, three...." He mouthed the words *two* and *one* before pointing at Francesca to go ahead.

"We're back with Beau Davis from the Inevitable Thorns, and we're now also joined by Jamie Griffin. Jamie shot to fame earlier this year when the video of a dance he choreographed featuring two men went viral. Jamie and his dance partner have now joined the Inevitable Thorns European tour, and Beau and Jamie have found a romance of their own."

Francesca shot us a handful of questions designed to make the audience swoon and feel like they were getting the inside scoop into our relationship. She also asked about my dance background and the "Galaxies" choreography itself, which impressed me. It would be so easy to paint me in a mere boyfriend role. The fact that she appeared to value my work was flattering. Overall, the interview went smashingly well. It was a risk for us to take so soon after the photo and Beau's dad's fiasco, but it paid off and allowed us to use our own voices. I only hoped that the interest in us would die off as fast as it began so we could go back to concentrating on the last remaining weeks of tour dates.

Beau

IT was finally here. The last night of the tour. It had been an insane eight months that had changed my life in so many ways. I had seen sights and places that I had only ever dreamed of visiting. My worldview had increased dramatically since visiting cities with thousands of years of history. After having a rocky time writing this album last summer, Thorns had come out the other side and triumphed with this catalog of new songs. We had showcased them throughout Europe for thousands of fans who didn't even speak our language. The band was stronger and more cohesive than ever, and we were all looking forward to our well-deserved break.

After we got through this last performance of course.

I didn't know exactly what the future held for Jamie and me. Life was easier when we were on tour and we didn't have to think about how to see each other next. We were together twenty-four seven, and if that wasn't a true test of a relationship, I had no idea what would be. Things between us grew stronger each day, and I knew that even if our careers kept us physically separated for a while, being with him would be worth it. I trusted our relationship in a way I never had with anyone else before.

Carter set up the opening to "Galaxies" for the final time. I was sure that the song would live on and Jamie's beautiful choreography would probably continue to be danced. But it would never be exactly the same. In all likelihood, it would never be performed live by the two of us together again.

The lights dimmed so Jamie and Hayden could step into their positions. The crowd went wild. I took a breath and began to play.

Since Jamie and Hayden had joined the tour, I found myself barely paying attention to my own performance of the song. My fingers knew what they needed to do. My eyes relished the opportunity to feast on the extraordinary display of strength and art directly in front of me on the stage.

I had never quite gotten over the image of Jamie in those tiny lavender-colored shorts he insisted on wearing in this piece. The whole thing messed with my head because he was so fucking hot in them, yet it also went beyond that. In some ways I barely even noticed he was nearly naked because I couldn't stop looking at the beautiful way his muscles moved. But the movements were also incredibly sexy in their own right. It was like I didn't know whether to be turned on or to break down and cry from how gorgeous it was.

As my favorite point in the song approached, I watched Jamie as he advanced toward the edge of the stage and then turned away from the audience to face Hayden—and therefore the band. He brought his leg way out behind him, reaching for his imagined lover in desperation. I asked him about that moment one day, and Jamie had told me that the position was called an arabesque. The angle of his head shifted slightly, almost imperceptibly to anyone who wasn't looking for it or wasn't as familiar with the moment as I was. Jamie's gaze met mine, and I could see his face was covered in a stream of tears.

Like the professional he was, Jamie managed to keep it together for the rest of the number. If anything, his emotion added to the dance and made it even more powerful. The song swelled to its conclusion, and I watched Hayden exit for the final time. I honestly wasn't sure what triggered it, if it was observing Hayden in the role of my former lover leave our stage forever, or if it was seeing Jamie—playing me—have such an emotional reaction. Either way, in that moment I had an epiphany about the music I had written nearly a year ago.

The song wasn't only about Dylan. It was also about my mom. And my dad. My brother, my ex-girlfriend Laura, and everyone else who had left or abandoned me due to whatever the circumstances were. That's why I had been hesitant to include pronouns in the lyrics. That's why the lyrics were so general instead of mentioning specifics. I had always attributed it to protecting Dylan's privacy, but I realized in that moment that subconsciously it went far deeper than that. On the first day I met Jamie, I hadn't given him a straight answer as to whether Hayden's character comes back or hope remains at the end of the song. I had been reluctant to admit that I wasn't optimistic about Dylan. But now I thought maybe hope did remain for the bigger picture, for my world beyond any individual circumstance. And most of all, for the life I was building with Jamie.

Oblivious to my internal awakening, Jamie winked at me as he took his final steps off the stage to overwhelming applause. I would get Jamie's thoughts on it later. We had time.

The show carried on after the dance, soaring through the songs on an epic heartbeat as we gave the audience our all. The four of us together were unstoppable. A force to reckon with. My band of brothers, who could get me through anything. Once we were done with this performance, we would each need to take stock and figure out who we were outside the band. Ultimately we would find our way back together, but we would be individuals instead of a collective in the meantime. Dean and Ash would visit with their families. Carter would go home to Chase. There was only one person I wanted to spend my time off with. And from the way he was grinning at me from the wings, I hoped like hell he felt the same way.

The final note faded, and the roar was incredible. The four of us let out a collective burst of laughter and met in the center of the stage, as we always did, to say our goodbyes. I flung my arms around Carter and Dean, throwing Ash a smile on Carter's other side. The entire arena was on their feet, yelling and stomping and applauding. Cory, Hayden, and Jamie were standing beside each other in the wings, and Ash gestured for them to join us for one more bow.

Or so almost everyone thought.

"So," Dean said into Carter's main microphone, causing a hush to fall over the crowd. "Normally that'd be it. We're not big on encores or any of that, but tonight we have something a little different cooked up. When I heard we'd have dancers joining us on this tour, I made one request to Jamie on their first night with us."

An enthusiastic cheer began in the audience. They had no idea what was going on, but they knew it was bound to be something special.

"Boys?" Dean rallied us.

Ash, Dean, and I returned to our instruments. Jamie grabbed an unknowing Hayden to come stand next to my keyboard with him. Cory hightailed it off the stage before he got roped into participating in the spectacle.

"Oh God," Hayden whispered. "Is this what I think it is?"

"Absolutely it is!" I replied.

The volume of the fans was insane, and they still had no idea what awaited them. Carter looked backward to us from his microphone and raised his hands in the air in a sign of triumph. We had fucking done it.

He turned to face the crowd and cupped the mic between both hands and began to sing the most epically profound song to end the tour with—"(I've Had) The Time of My Life."

Jamie

HAYDEN and I watched together on the side while the Thorns kicked it into high gear. Thorns didn't play a lot of covers, but Beau and the rest of the guys seemed comfortable and had obviously found time to practice this song once or twice in secret.

I reflected on my life over the past few months while I stared at Beau, an overwhelming calm washing over me. Everything that had happened to me recently was because of this man. I trusted my own training, talent, and vision, but the lucky break of my career had been meeting and talking with Beau. He had brought my artistic voice into the limelight. He had given me back my ability to dance. I had no ridiculous notion that I would be able to dance professionally again; hell, some nights even the one number seemed to be all my ankle could take. But Beau had found a way to give me something that had been taken before I could really even learn to appreciate it. It started as a physical thing with us—intended to be a one-night stand—but he had become so much more. I wanted him in my life after the tour. Permanently if he would have me.

I geared up for the big moment. Dean met my gaze, and we nodded to each other. He quickly stripped off his bass guitar, handing it to Cory in the wings. Carter picked up the mic stand and shuffled slightly to one side so I could move into his position at the center of the stage. I gave Dean the signal at the perfect moment in the music, and he ran flying at me from the side. The crowd was in absolute hysterics as I positioned my hands on Dean's hips and lifted him high above my head. Camera flashes came at us from every angle as it seemed like every person in the audience wanted a picture of this ridiculous moment. Dean was the perfect Baby, throwing his arms out to the sides and holding tension in his body like I had taught him in our daily ballet classes. I was shocked that he had committed to keeping up the daily routine. He had actually been a pretty receptive student and had mentioned on several occasions he felt healthier and more flexible. While Dean got painted as the party-boy class clown, he was actually a pretty cool guy, and I'd been happy we had gotten to know each other a little.

I lowered Dean down before my arms gave out— dude was *heavy* for such a skinny guy. Glancing to my left, I saw Carter wiping his eyes from laughter as he barely kept it together enough to sing the vocals. Dean and I did some sort of impromptu bro-handshake thing before he went to retrieve his bass and finish the song. Beau shot me a wink as I made my way back over to his keyboard to stand between him and Hayden like nothing had happened.

The song ended, and once again the band plus Hayden and I made our way up to the front of the stage. As we started to walk, Beau slipped his hand into mine. I stared at our linked fingers—in front of this crowd of thousands who would undoubtedly pick up on the gesture.

We smiled at each other as we joined the rest of the guys and took one final bow.

Beau

THE end of the show had come and gone. Jamie and Dean's little hijinks went exactly as planned, and it would surely be the moment we all remembered from our last night on tour. I thought the relationship they had formed was adorable. To be honest, I loved that Jamie had bonded with each one of my band brothers. He fit in with us in a way that few other people would. Jamie was dedicated and hardworking, though he knew how to laugh and enjoy the ride as well.

The crew was done loading out our stage for the last time, and the rest of the band was already on their way back to the hotel. I had created my own little ritual of being the last one out of the venue at the end of tour, which the guys all knew and respected. For some reason I liked to soak in the quiet of the theater or arena after all the mayhem.

Looking out over the empty rows of seats. It was a moment of solitude, a way to reflect on the whole experience and how I had grown from it personally and musically.

"Galaxies" began to fade in softly through the house speaker system. It was so quiet to begin with, I barely knew it was real and not a figment of my imagination. The lighting shifted, and I was suddenly surrounded by a stage full of stars, slowly spinning around me. It was probably a mirror ball, but whatever. Stars.

"Dance with me, rock star?"

Jamie appeared from behind me, his hand raised and a half smile on his lips. He was dressed in jeans, which he didn't normally wear, and had on an unbuttoned suit jacket over a white button-down. My pulse sped up at the sight of him. He was so beautiful. So effortlessly romantic with the gesture.

I nodded and met him in the center of the stage. He took my right hand in his, holding the small of my back with the other. My nose found the nape of his neck, smelling the freshly washed scent of his skin. Jamie led the dance, holding me tightly and directing my movements with the simple pressure of his fingers on my back. I couldn't remember the last time I had slow danced with someone. Between the simple rocking motion and the feeling of him against me, it was soothing. I didn't have to think, didn't have to do anything other than follow where he led me. The tiny beams of light from the mirror ball twirled around us in the darkness, reminding me of the night in Galway spent looking at the stars. The night before the photo of us leaked and everything became real.

I read once that due to the vastness of space, crashes between stars are incredibly rare. It's thought that in our galaxy, a stellar collision may only happen once every

10,000 years. The unlikelihood of two objects flying through the empty cosmos, meeting in the exact same location, is exorbitantly low. The universe is a mess of gravity and physics, of supernovas and black holes, of where we've been and where we're going. Of music and dance. There's a lot of random out there, but I'm a firm believer that some collisions happen for a reason.

"I love you, Beau," Jamie murmured in my ear.

The song ended as I was lost in the emotion of being in Jamie's arms. We kept spinning in the silence, the two of us in our own world. Alone in the galaxy. I almost didn't want to say the words back and risk breaking the silence of the moment. He pulled away from me slightly and looked into my eyes.

"Meeting you changed my life. It changed *everything*. I know we're still getting to know each other, and we don't know what's coming next, but I want to figure it out together."

I took in his words, knowing I wanted that too. I wanted the long talks, the lazy strolls, the late-night breakfasts. I wanted the intimacy and the breathtaking sex. I wanted the joint creativity, the songs. The dances.

I wanted him.

I had known that for so long, yet there had always been my underlying fear of what would happen next. What had happened before with others. Am I too desperate? Will he leave me? Now, suddenly, things seemed simple. Jamie helped me become stronger, resilient, more self-confident. He made me happier. I loved him for everything he was and everything he made me.

"I love you too," I whispered.

He pulled me back into his arms slowly, and we continued to dance together in the quiet, empty theater.

Under the stars.

**DREAMSPUN
DESIRES**

Now Available
Next to Me

An Inevitable Duets Romance

Can an awkward student and a closeted rock star make beautiful music together?

Music composition student Chase Collins has always worn his heart on his sleeve. That's why it was so quick to break in high school when Chase lost Carter West, his best friend and first love, to an ill-fated kiss.

Imagine Chase's surprise five years later when Carter, now a rising rock star, admits to the world that Chase inspired his band's award-winning song—and that Carter was in love with him all along.

Frontman Carter West has been closeted his whole life. Now that he's out in the most public way possible, he can finally indulge in the romantic impulses he's always had to keep stifled. Reconnecting with Chase gives him the opportunity to explore a whole new side of himself.

But the next tour draws inevitably closer, and Chase is wary. Carter left Chase once before. Can two gifted musicians write themselves a love song that will last a lifetime?

www.dreamspinnerpress.com

www.ingramcontent.com/pod-product-compliance
Lightning Source LLC
Chambersburg PA
CBHW030303200626
46816CB00002BA/746